In love with the connect

Ebony Diamonds

Copyright © 2020 Ebony Turrentine

Contents

Chapter 1

Bella Deverou

"Have you lost your fucking mind?" Drew said, clocking me upside the head for the fifth time since we had been home.

I tried to fight off his reign of terror, but he was too strong for me. This man beat on me like I was a grown man and then was quick to apologize when I said I was leaving, only for him to do the shit again. I stopped believing him a long time ago. I knew it wouldn't end until he killed me, and I didn't want that at all. Tonight's beating was about me smiling at one of his friends too hard at the 'show your bitch and money' parties he and his friends threw all the time. My man was a drug dealer and a good one at that. He just couldn't be a good man to save his life. The love I once had turned into pure hate and I couldn't wait to rid myself of him and move the fuck on with my life. That was easier said than done because he always said if he couldn't have me then he would have to kill me to make sure nobody else could. I believed him because one day I packed my stuff and tried to go and he smacked me in the head with a baseball bat, leaving me in a coma for a week. He came to the hospital apologizing and begging my forgiveness and me, being stupid and frightened, I went back.

"Bella! You hear me bitch!"

I didn't respond, which made him even madder. I tried my best to protect my stomach since I was pregnant with our first child, but I couldn't stop him from kicking me in the stomach and back. I felt a sharp pain and I knew we were about to lose our baby.

"Drew, please, you're hurting the baby," was the last thing I said before he stomped me in the face, and I blacked out.

I'm Bella Deverou. Yes, I'm that stupid bitch you talk to your friends about, the stupid bitch that would allow a man to bring her down to a level of self-hatred, and the type of stupid bitch that would let a man beat her ass and almost kill her then be under him while he fucked her brains, allowing to him to come back. I didn't choose the shit it just happened, and I couldn't seem to get out.

I'm 25 and never worked a day in my life. My father was a top dude in the streets of Miami and he always made sure his princess had everything she needed and that's how I met Drew. He worked for my father and he would always snoop around me, charming me and making me fall in love with him. That was my mistake. After he took my virginity, he had it in his mind that he owned me. Since I was young, I thought it was cute that he was possessive, but over the years it had gotten deadly. He beats me anytime he feels like it and sometimes I don't even need to give him a reason.

I keep trying to figure out what I did wrong, but I knew it was just his malicious nature. All I needed was a chance to leave, but since he never left me alone, I never got it. I had nobody but his friend's girlfriends and most of them were going through the same thing I was. My father was in jail now and my mother died in a car accident when I was a teen. I was alone with a monster and the nightmare was only beginning. The first time he ever hit me was when I was in the store getting him a pack of swishers. A high school friend named Mike came in and I gave him a hug. Drew walked in and saw this, and he acted like he was cool, dapping Mike up and all. When we got back to his house, he beat me for almost two hours and knocked out my front tooth.He told me I disrespected him and that if I wanted to live, I better not do that again. I had no idea what he was talking about. I had to get my tooth replaced and I told my father some girls jumped me. I knew he would have killed Drew, so I kept quiet.

I don't know how much longer I could survive him. Every time it seemed to get worse and worse. I would often cry when I knew he was on the way home because I already prepared myself to get beat up. I hated how I felt afterward. All the pain and then the soreness and then I heal only to be beaten and bruised again. I started pretending to be sleep when he came home because I didn't want to even breathe too hard, but that didn't stop him. He would hit me and wake me out of my sleep to complain about one thing or another. I just needed some help. Somebody please help me.

"Ms. Deverou, can you hear me?"

I started to open my eyes and saw that I was in a hospital room.

"What...happened?" I struggled to talk. I was in so much pain and my neck was in a brace.

"Well, the police found you on the side of the road. They will be back to talk to you about what happened. The detective ran downstairs, but he will be back."

I started crying. This bastard put me on the side of the road to die.

"I have some bad news for you as well. You miscarried and there was nothing we could do to stop it."

I cried even harder.

The door opened and a dark-skinned handsome man came in with a nice suit.

"Hi, Ms. Deverou. I'm Detective Lawson. Can you tell me what happened to you?"

I attempted to shake my head, but the brace stopped me. "No, I don't." I closed my eyes fighting the pain it caused to speak.

"Well, we won't charge you for the vials of dope we found on you because somehow it got lost on the way to evidence. You're far too young to throw your life away using that shit."

I was confused; I never used dope in my life. "I don't do drugs, sir. I have no idea what you're talking about."

He came over and grabbed my arm and turned it over. He pointed at one spot and looked at me. "Well, you had it in your system, and you have a needle prick in your arm."

I covered my mouth with my hand. Drew shot me with dope and put the shit on me. I was more hurt than I had ever been in all my years with him. I was more hurt than when he fucked my best friend and had a baby with her years ago, more hurt than when he called me home just so I could find him fucking some hoe in our bed, even more hurt than when he pushed me out of the window and I almost broke my neck. He knew I was pregnant, and he beat me and shot me up with dope, leaving me for dead. I hated that man with all my soul.

"Please, just leave," I said, crying harder.

I sat in bed for three weeks and prayed that I would just die to end this misery. I couldn't even fathom the fact that the man I thought I loved treated me like less than a dog. I just watched TV and tried to heal. I made up my mind that I was leaving him for good and would never look back. I heard a knock on my door, and I told the person to come in. It was Peaches, the only one of the crew's girlfriend I clicked with on a friendship level.

"Hey, boo, how you feeling today?" she said, kissing my cheek and sitting down next to me. She put her hand on mines and I started crying. Peaches grabbed a napkin and wiped my tears for me. She was sweet like that.

"I'm as good as can be expected, Peaches. Have you seen Drew?"

She turned away and put her head down. "Yes, he's been partying and acting like you're not laid her in this hospital."

Of course, he was. "I'm leaving tomorrow, and I have nowhere to go," I said, probably sounding pathetic.

"Well, you know I stash all my money from Bizzy so I can give you some cash until you get on your feet. You know I don't mind."

She was so cool for that shit. She was in the same situation, but she fought back, and he stopped after she shot him. He never hit her again.

"Thanks, Peaches, you don't know how much that shit means to me."

We chatted for a little while longer, but she had to go pick her son up from daycare. She wrote me a check for $10,000 and told me if I needed more to call her. I was left alone again. I guess a hotel room would due for now until I got my own.

I was released the next day and I dreaded going home to get my clothes. I still had my car keys, so I was happy to at least have a whip. When I got to our house, I was so happy Drew wasn't home and I ran in as quickly as possible to collect some things. I got my suitcase and started stuffing clothes and anything else I would need and started to leave. I was leaving out the door when I heard a car pull up and I knew it was Drew. I almost pissed on myself I was so scared. I hurried out the door and he ran over and kicked the suitcase out of my hand.

"Where the fuck you think you going?"

Before I could answer, a blonde white girl got out of his car and she was looking at me like she wasn't wrong for being with my man. She could have his ass. Let him use her as a punching bag.

"I'm leaving. You made me lose our baby and had me in the hospital for three fucking weeks while you partied and fucked these nasty ass bitches," I said, directing that toward the white girl.

"I told you that you weren't leaving me, Bella, unless you were dead. Get the fuck in the house."

I made a dash down the driveway and he caught me and pulled me by my hair back into the house.

"Stop it! Why can't you just let me leave? You have somebody else here already. Please, just let me go."

He continued to drag me and threw me down the basement steps. "You belong to me. Nobody will ever touch you as long as I live." He slammed the door and I was on the concrete hurting from the fall.

I went to the back door and he was standing there with a hammer and nails, pounding until it was nailed shut. I went to the family room and sat on the couch crying. I started hearing moans like somebody was having sex. How could he be so cruel to me? I never did anything to deserve any of this. The basement door flew open and I ran into a corner and balled up.

"Get the fuck over here, Bella!" he screamed.

I didn't budge. He came and grabbed me and dragged me up the steps. The white girl was ass naked lying on my living room sofa.

"This is my friend, Heather. She wanted to know if you were into threesomes. By the way, you can take some advice from her 'cause she took the dick like a champ."

This nigga and this bitch have lost their minds. I spit at her and Drew punched me in the face, dropping me, and I could hear the bitch laugh.

"Bitch, you don't know how to act to save your fucking life."

I don't know how but I found the strength to knee him in his balls and I broke for the door as fast as I could. Not fast enough. He pulled me back and he took my pants off. The bitch was watching and playing with herself as Drew stuck his fingers inside me. He pulled his hand out and it had blood on it because I was still bleeding from the miscarriage.

"You nasty bitch," he said.

I could hear him spit in his hand and he spread my ass and put his dick into my butthole.

"OOOOWWWW. Drew, stop it that hurts."

He was grunting and being as rough as he could. "Yeah, look at her. She can't take it in the ass like you, Heather."

I heard her laugh. "I see. I guess that's why you needed a real woman, huh?"

I got so mad that he was doing this to me. He just couldn't stop torturing me. After he came inside my ass, he left me there.

"Get dressed and go the fuck back downstairs. Matter of fact, get me and Heather something to drink and grab us some food too."

I pulled my pants up and pretended to walk away. I found the courage to kick him in the nuts and run. I didn't look back as I ran and grabbed the suitcase that was still in the lawn. I jumped in my car, fumbling with my keys. He came out with his dick swinging and started to run towards the car. I finally got it started and I zoomed in reverse out of the driveway and sped off.

"IM FREE!" I screamed and laughed.

I drove to South Beach and found a little hotel to stay in. I didn't cash the check from Peaches yet, but I was going to do it first thing in the morning. I was still scared he would find me so I planned to move hotels every few days. I went to the ATM and withdrew as much cash from my cards as I could because I knew Drew would cut them off soon, so I took advantage. I grabbed some Cuban food and since I didn't have a phone, I grabbed a burner cell. I knew Peaches' number by heart, so I called her immediately and told her what happened. She told me Drew called Bizzy to see if I was there. I begged her not to say anything about speaking to me and I knew she wouldn't because that was just her nature. I looked in the mirror at myself and saw my once beautiful face drained and painted with a black eye. I would never be with another man like him and I was determined to find my own way.

Chapter 2

I woke up feeling slightly refreshed and feeling like I had a huge weight lifted off my shoulders. For the first time in a long time, I didn't wake up feeling like I should have died in my sleep. I looked around the tiny hotel room and made a pact with myself that I would get a job and make my own way, never depending on another nigga again. I went to the bank and cashed the check Peaches gave me. I decided to open up an account and put all the money in it. Since I didn't have an address I told them I would use my instant debit until further notice. When I left the bank, a guy approached me from behind and asked me if I had a man. When I turned around he bucked his head back. I knew my eye looked bad and I was embarrassed by my appearance, so I went and got some concealer and a pair of sunglasses. I felt so good that nothing could stop my feeling of freedom that is until I walked into Wal-Mart to get some toiletries.

I was walking down the aisle minding my business when I ran into my old best friend, Asia. She had her baby with her and I pretended not to see her at first.

"Hey, Bella," she said like we were on some good note and she could speak to me.

I didn't say shit and started looking at toothpaste.

"Bella, I know you're still hurting, but the shit just happened. I can't say anything else."

I laughed and looked at her then the little girl. "Then don't, bitch. By the way, you can have that nigga on a platter as long as you keep him the fuck away from me. Bye, hoe."

I turned my back to her and saw her looking at me and she walked off. I rounded the corner to get body wash and I could hear Asia's voice. She must have been on the phone because it was one sided from what I can hear.

"Yes, she here now. She said I can have you and that you were done...are you serious? She had an abortion without you knowing?" I knew she was on the phone with Drew.

I walked right up and snatched her phone. "Really nigga? I had an abortion? You kicked our baby out of me and shot me up with dope, remember that?" I didn't even let him answer. I smashed her phone on the ground and stomped it. She was scared as shit too. "Now run and tell that, bitch!" I went and paid for my shit so I could leave just in case he showed up.

I couldn't have been anymore pissed that he was telling people I had an abortion. I got in my car and left. As I drove down Bay Road I saw a small apartment building and it had a "for rent" sign for a one bedroom for $900 a month. With the money I took from my cards and the money Peaches gave me I could be okay for a few months or at least until I found a job. I pulled over and went to the brown door that said rental office. I walked in and there was a fat guy sitting at the desk smoking a cigar. I pushed the smoke out of my face and he tapped it out.

"How can I help you, pretty lady?" he said sitting back and making a disgusting grunting noise.

"I wanted to know about the apartment for rent. Can I see it?"

He got his fat ass up and went to grab the keys from a wooden board that was behind him. "Come on."

I followed him to the apartment on the first floor. It was small but perfect for me since I was alone.

"I don't ask for much except that you pay your rent on time and don't make a lot of noise," he said, watching me walk around.

"Ok, so what do I have to do?"

He waved his hand telling me to follow him out. When we got back into the office he pulled out a stack of papers and flipped through them until he found the one he was looking for.

"I just need you to give me first month and last and you're in. I don't do all the background and credit check shit."

I was excited to hear that. This is my first place and I was happier than a fat kid with a bag of chocolate. I told him I would be right back and I went to the bank and withdrew $2,000 and hurried back.

"Ok, sign this and here are your keys."

Damn that was easy. I thought I would have to have paystubs and shit. I ain't questioning it, though. I went back into my new place and looked around. It was the beginning for me and I was too excited.

I didn't have money for a lot of stuff to furnish, but I made it work. I bought a twin bed and a TV so I could at least lay my head somewhere. I got a DVD player and brought a few movies to watch as well. I may not have had shit, but I was comfy being alone and away from that piece of shit. My phone started ringing and it was Peaches. Of course it was her because nobody else had this number.

"Hey, honey, what you doing?" she said. I could hear lil' Bizzy in the background making noise.

"Nothing much. Guess what? I got me an apartment."

She let out a scream. "Yes bitch, that's what I'm talking about. Set your life up, boo. I gotta come over. Can I come tonight?" she asked.

"Bitch, of course. Bring some gas too. I need to smoke bad and I'm going to get us a bottle."

"That's a bet, Bella. Look, text me the address and I will be there around eight."

We said goodbye and I texted her. I couldn't wait to kick it with my homie. I got in the car and headed to Miami Liquor. I always went there because of their selection. I walked in and immediately picked up a bottle of Remy and a bottle of Moet. I didn't know what I was in the mood for I chose them both. I grabbed some glasses while I was there since I didn't have any dishes. I went to pay for my stuff and when I handed the guy the bills, he told me I had a $200 credit form the guy who just left out. I didn't even notice anybody else in the store. He handed me back the change and I ran outside to thank the stranger. When I saw a dude getting into a brand-new Challenger, I knew it must have been him.

"Hey!"

He looked up and I recognized him and got frightened. I started to walk off and I heard him run up and he tapped my shoulder.

"You were calling for me, right? Why you run away?"

I looked around to make sure Drew wasn't anywhere near. "I just wanted to say thanks and give you the money back."

He smiled and lord was he sexy. He stood about 6'4" and had a cute little mole under his right eye.He was Drew's connect. I met him numerous times and I just knew he would tell Drew he saw me.

"You Drew's girl, right?"

I closed my eyes and I don't know why but I started to cry.

"What's wrong? It's just liquor."

I cracked a smile at his stupid joke. "I just don't want Drew to know where I am."

He shook his head. "I heard about him and how he treats you. You don't have to deal with that shit."

I wiped the tears from my eyes, and he grabbed my hand and wiped them away for me. I felt this sensation, but I wasn't ready. "I left him and that's why I don't want you to tell him," I said starting to walk away.

"Hey, take my number in case you need anything. I knew your father and I know he wouldn't want you to be out here with no help."

I was a little hesitant, but when he brought up my father I just went ahead and put his number in my phone.

"Text me so I can save your number." I texted my name and we said goodbye.

I saw him looking in his phone probably putting my number in it. I didn't remember his name, so I just put "Connect." I drove home thinking about him and how pleasant he was to me. That's how Drew started off too. I pushed any thoughts of attraction to him out of my mind and continued my evening. Peaches came as promised and she offered to get me some furniture then she wrote me another check. This time it was fifty g's. She had that and then some because of who her nigga, Bizzy, was. He was kingpin in Miami and on the same level as Drew. Money-making pieces of shit. My bank account was like that too I just didn't know if I had been cut off yet. In fact, I made a mental note to check accounts in the morning so see if I still could get some money.

The next morning, I deposited the check in the bank and then went to Wells Fargo to check my accounts. This nigga must have forgot because one still had over $100,000 in it and the savings had almost $200,000. I emptied them and walked out with cashier's checks and deposited those into the new account. *If I had known, I would have gotten a better apartment,* I laughed to myself. Damn look how God looks how for people too stupid to look out for themselves. I also got a cashier's check for $60,000 so I could give Peaches her money back. I went to CB2 on Jefferson Street. I wanted to get some furniture so I would look like I lived in a bachelorette pad. I bought a black and gray sofa and loveseat with granite tables to match. My bedroom set was canopy sleigh bed with two dressers and an ottoman. I didn't need a dining room set since I didn't have a separate dining area. I did have a breakfast bar in the window of the kitchen, so I got two bar stools. They were going to deliver it later that night, so I hurriedly went to the store and ended up spending a lot of money on my furnishings. I got pictures, vases, and more shit than I could fit in my car. The thing was packed, and I should have thought about how the fuck I was going to get this shit in by myself. I started taking them in when my phone rung and it read "Connect." I didn't answer it because I was trying to get this shit in the house. I didn't know what the hell he would be calling me for anyway. I wasn't looking for any friends and I damn sure wasn't looking for a man after the bullshit I went through with Drew.

My home was furnished, I had money, and these last

few days where bliss. I hadn't been beaten in days and the sad part is it that didn't feel normal. I was used to getting fucked up on a daily basis and that shit was a sad reality. I started crying when I went into the bathroom and saw the bruises on my stomach and sides. I had flashbacks of all the suffering and pain my heart felt with tears flowing for what seemed like hours. I felt purged when I got off the bathroom floor and I decided to smoke up and have a few drinks. It just felt good to relax without the fear of being punished for breathing. I rolled a nice ass jay and lay on the couch, enjoying the nothingness. I didn't have cable yet so I put on *Bridget Jones's Diary* and dozed off. When I woke up I had two missed calls. One from Peaches and one from the connect. I didn't have a clue why he kept calling, but I wished had I never texted him. I decided to call back and he answered on the first ring.

"How you doing, Ms. Lady? I just wanted to check on you, but I see you was ignoring a nigga."

I was kind of embarrassed when he said that, so I lied. "I was kind of busy, but I meant to call back. So, what's up?"

He laughed and I could hear people talking in the background. "I just wanted to check on you. I kind of been thinking about you because of the way you started crying the other day."

That was nice of him, I thought to myself.

"Well, I'm fine. Thanks for checking on me. I'm sorry, I don't know your name."

He laughed me off. "You just hurt my feelings, girl. It's Domo."

"Ok, well, thank you, Domo, and I didn't mean to hurt your feelings," I said even though I knew he was just flirting with me.

"Let me ask you something. Since you left Drew, do you know what you're gonna do for cash?"

"I guess I just have to get a job. I was going to start looking tomorrow."

"Well, I need a secretary for my construction company and I thought you may be interested. I can start you off at $25 an hour is that's cool. I hate to see you out here struggling."

I had a nice chunk of change but it would last forever, so that sounded damn good. I wouldn't have known he had a company. He was just a dope dealer to me.

"Ok, but I don't know how do nothing so don't be mad at me. I'm a fast learner, though," I stated in an eager tone.

"Ok, since it's Thursday you can start Monday. I can text you the address and be there at eight."

I was so excited. I never had a job before; I just got my first one and it was paying bank.

"Ok, thanks, Domo."

"Say it again."

I was confused. "Say what?"

"My name. It sounded so sexy I need to hear it again."

Oh no, let me stop this shit right here. "Thank you for the opportunity, but let's keep it strictly business. I just left something that my heart hasn't healed from. I will see you Monday."

I hung up. His voice was so deep and smooth that I wanted to say it again, but I just can't take the chance on dealing with another street nigga and I ending up fucked up all over again.

***

It was Friday and I wanted to visit my dad. I couldn't

dare tell him what I allowed Drew to do to me, so I planned on pretending everything was fine. I went through the search and waited for them to come tell me to come back. It took forever and they finally called me. I walked to the table and sat down. My father still looked good for his age and even though he was locked up he didn't let it beat him down.

"Hey, Papa, you looking good."

He smiled and then frowned. "What the fuck happened to your eye?"

I guess the concealer didn't work as well as I hoped. "Nothing, Papa, I just got into some shit. You know bitches stay hating on me," I lied.

"You always seem to be getting fucked up by some females. You telling me the truth?" I diverted my eyes down to the table. "That muthafucka been hitting you, hasn't he?"

I started to cry and nodded. I couldn't tell him everything because I knew what would happen. "Just this once, but I left him, and I got my own place and everything."

He slammed his fist on the table and the guards walked over. He put his hands up to show them everything was okay. "Why the hell you ain't tell me, Bella? You knew I would have got his ass laid the fuck out."

I wiped my face. "Because I don't want you doing that type of stuff no more. Let's just forget about this and enjoy the visit."

He flared his nostrils and had an evil look in his eyes. I knew he wasn't done.

"I got a job with a guy named Domo."

He scrunched his face like the name sounded familiar. "You talking about 'tall' Domo? Dark nigga?"

I nodded my head yes.

He nodded in approval. "I knew him when he was younger. His father was the plug and I heard he running shit like his old man." I didn't answer that because it was none of my business.

"How far along are you now? Your stomach is still flat."

I almost choked up at the thought of my miscarriage and how it came about. "I lost it, Papa."

He had a sad look. "Damn, girl, you got a lot going on. Listen here: I don't want you going back to that clown. If I even hear you been with him we gonna have problems."

I took him very seriously. My father wasn't a man to play with. We continued our visit and said our goodbyes. I missed him and he still had three more years to go, so it would be a while before he was free again.

When I left the prison, I couldn't help but think about Domo. I wished I could have met him before Drew and maybe things would have been different. I didn't get any bad vibes about him, but I guess I'm not the best judge of character anyway.

I didn't know what I was supposed to wear to work, so I went to Macy's and got myself some professional looking clothes. My ass was so fat that no matter what I wore I looked like a fully dressed thot. I was blessed and I guess I couldn't hide the shit for nothing. I went to Best Buy after I left Macy's to buy a laptop and a tablet. I needed to figure out what the hell I needed to know before I went in and made an ass of myself. When I got home, I researched typing skills and how to be an efficient assistant. I couldn't type for shit, so I got a program to help me learn. I used my index fingers to press the buttons and got frustrated when I couldn't remember where they were. I stopped and realized I watched every DVD I had. I was using public Wi-Fi so

I decided so just go online and order cable so I could have my own and be able to watch some damn TV. I got Netflix, hooked my laptop up to the TV, and stayed in the house the whole weekend chilling.

***

Monday couldn't get here fast enough. I was ready and after trying to learn to type all weekend I just wanted to get the shit over with. Domo texted me the address and I was way passed impressed when I got to his building. I went into the luxurious lobby and stopped at the front desk.

"I'm here to see Domo."

The security looked at each other and laughed. "You ain't the only one. He got y'all dickmatized, huh?"

I was offended and curious by what he said. "Excuse me? I'm here to start my new job. I think you're very unprofessional and I will be letting him know his security is a bunch of disrespectful motherfuckers."

They had fear now. I guess the thought of them losing their jobs brought them back to reality. "Here's a pass and I'm sorry for that."

I snatched it and saw it said the 16th floor. I got on the elevator and swayed to the song they used for elevator music. It was Lauryn Hill. I had never been on an elevator that played R&B. That was some smooth shit. I got off and went to the door that read Dominic Birkdale. I figured Domo was short for Dominic. When I walked in there was a desk with a computer and a phone. I guess that was mines. I went and knocked on the large oakwood door and I heard moaning.

"Give me a minute," I heard Domo say. I recognized his voice because of course I could never forget something so sexy.

"Damn, daddy. Yes, fuck me, baby."

I backed away from the door and left out. I was jealous and I didn't know why. I didn't want him; I didn't want anything to do with him besides work. Why did I feel that way? I went to press the elevator and the door to the office opened. A beautiful woman emerged sweaty and obviously satisfied by the look on her face. The elevator got there just as Domo walked out and I hurried and got on.

"Bella, where you going?"

The woman looked at me and gave me a mean mug. I mugged her ass right back. "I think this was a mistake. Thank you for the chance, but I'm going to head home."

He saw something that I didn't mean to show: the jealousy in my eyes. He was holding the elevator door so I couldn't even make my escape.

"Baby, I will call you later," the girl said, attempting to kiss him, but his eyes were locked with mine.

She snapped in his face and he looked at her through squinted eyes. "Don't you see I'm talking? Matter of fact don't call me later. You just got on my nerves with that bullshit."

"Who the fuck you snapping at, shawty?"

She looked at me completely embarrassed from the way he just dug into her ass. She smacked her teeth and walked to the staircase.

"Come on and stop being silly. I got your desk all setup for you."

I got off and followed him to the office and sat my bag on the desk. "So, what do you want me to do first?"

"Do you like flowers?" he asked, writing on a sticky note.

"I guess, but I don't think it's appropriate for you to be giving me flowers."

He looked up at me and smirked. "They weren't for you. I just wanted to know if that was a nice gift to apologize to someone."

My face was tighter than an ass hole when he said that.

He handed me the paper he had scribbled on. "Send those to Ja'Tori Johnson. All the local numbers are in your binder in the drawer on the bottom."

He turned and walked in and closed his door. Well that was embarrassing. I ordered the flowers and he came out with his wallet in his hand.

"I gotta run out for a second. Can you grab the files off my desk and organize them? I also need you to familiarize yourself with that Rolodex. It's a lot of high-end clients and I need you be on the money with them."

My face was still on the floor from earlier, so I didn't even look at him and I pretended to be going through some binder on the desk. "Ok, I got you."

He hadn't moved so I looked up. He reached down and touched my eye. I flinched; my nerves had been that bad from Drew.

"You deserve better than this," he said before leaving out and waiting on the elevator.

I felt his touch still on my face and his cologne took over my senses. I felt the tightening in my stomach, and I couldn't fight my attraction. I went to get the files off his desk and when I walked in, I was very impressed at his layout. It was so gentlemen like. I couldn't get over the fact that he was a dope dealer and he ran a nice business too. I rubbed my hand across his desk and thought about the noises ole girl was making earlier. It had me moist and I wondered what she was feeling when she was calling him "daddy." I looked out, saw the coast was clear, closed his door, and I sat in his large leather chair with my legs up on his desk.

I was happy I chose to wear the skirt. I massaged my clit until I had my pussy nice and creamy. I inhaled his cologne and wished like hell it was his tongue circling my clit. Those nice thick lips would feel like magic I bet. I finger fucked myself and was enjoying every bit of it. Just as I was cumming the door swung open and Domo stood there with his mouth wide open.

"Bella I forgot —" He stopped dead in his tracks.

"OH MY GOD!" I screamed out.

I couldn't stop myself from cumming and he stood there watching me cum all over his chair. I wanted to crawl under his desk and die.

"I guess you got bored, huh?" he laughed, coming in and closing the door.

I got up and walked around the desk about to get the fuck out of there and never see him again. "I'm sorry. Oh God, I'm so embarrassed," I said, rushing past him and grabbing my stuff.

"Excuse me, Bella, but you have seven more hours."

I looked at him and he was serious. He walked up to me and handed me a tissue.

"I thought I should just leave."

He shook his head and told me to come in the office. He grabbed an envelope and handed it to me. "Don't. You work here and we can keep that between us. I do worse so don't be embarrassed. Next time use the chaise. I'm sure it's more comfortable."

I couldn't believe what he was saying. He just made me feel so comfortable about masturbating in his office. I don't know what the hell I was thinking, but I would never again try it.

"I need to you to fill those out and get them back to me as soon as possible. I also have a company car for you. I don't know if you want it, but it's yours."

He was amazing. "Ok, and I'm sorry again," I said backing out.

"Stop apologizing to me. I kind of wished I could have been the one to make you cum like you did. But that's, how did you put it? 'Inappropriate.'"

I gave him a slight smile at his sarcasm and left out his office and went to my desk flushed. I started to fill out the W-4 forms and the direct deposit information. I was sitting there for hours when he came out. I didn't look at him just like earlier when I made an ass of myself. He reached over me to grab the rolodex and I felt the warmth of his body and my toes curled up.

"This is the best Dominican food you can get in Miami. I want you to order me the plantain, rice, and empanadas. Feel free to run up the bill on yourself. Get whatever you heart desires."

My heart desires you, I thought to myself. He stood there for a minute and I just went ahead and asked him, "Why are you being so nice to me? You want something right?"

He scrunched his eyebrows up and shook his head at me in pity. "It's heartbreaking when a beautiful young lady like yourself doesn't think she deserves anything but to be treated like a queen. I know you been through a lot, but just let me help you, baby...I mean Bella."

My heart dropped when he called me "baby." He was shooting electric currents through me and as emotionally damaged as I was, I couldn't believe I was feeling this way.

"I know, it's just you don't understand. I feel so worthless. I couldn't even protect our baby from him, and

I lost it after he beat me half to death."

He gritted his teeth and I saw anger in his eyes. Why does he even care? "Order lunch, and you can come and talk to me and get all this shit off your chest."

I nodded, fighting off the tears I always seem to muster up when I spoke about it. I ordered our food and when it arrived, I went in his office and we talked the whole time I was supposed to be working. I didn't do shit the whole rest of the day but tell him about all the bullshit that son of a bitch put me through. He insisted we have dinner, but I turned him down. I just wanted to go home and start today over.

***

The next day was much better. We hadn't even mentioned what happened the day before. I kicked myself in the ass for doing something so stupid on my first day of work. He was showing me everything that he wanted me to do for him. He was funny and very alluring. I could see why he had so many women fawning over him. He seemed to be the perfect catch. I loved his demeanor. He was so laid back and reserved that it was tantalizing. I had gotten good at my job and we had become friends. We had lunch every day together and sometimes we would leave and come back late from eating on the beach or something like that. Since he was the boss, we couldn't get in trouble for it. We would go to lunch with his clients or potential clients and he was such a gentleman that I really started feeling him. He gave me so much respect and it was like he wanted to make me happy. He made everything about me, and I was enjoying the attention. Sometimes he would bring me breakfast and the coffee would always be perfect.

******

1 month later

I sat at my desk looking over some papers for Domo when he came out his office door.

"You want to get some dinner? I mean since I'm your boss I'm ordering you to come join me."

I laughed and since of course I wasn't doing anything it was fine. "Ok that sounds good. Where we going?"

He waved his finger. "No, no, no, that's not how this relationship works, baby. You got to get used to being surprised who if you want to deal with me on a personal level."

He was so flirtatious. "Relationship, huh? I guess."

He smiled and went back into his office. I was blushing like crazy. I fanned myself with a piece of paper. After work, he told me that we were getting some seafood and I was ready for that. We went to Ocean Drive and ate at an outside bar and restaurant. I had a good time with him. He knew how to show me a good time. We were sitting at the table nice and full. I was finishing my last margarita when he asked me a question that turned me red all over.

"When is the last time you were touched Bella?"

I almost drowned myself when I choked off my drink. "Why?" I asked, laughing and trying to ease my giddiness.

"I just want to know. I mean you look like you need to relax a little."

I put my eyes down into my blue drink and I looked back up at him. "It's been a while since I actually wanted to be touched."

He stared me up and down which caused me to look

away.

"Dominic, baby, is that you?"

I saw one of the girls who frequented Domo's office.

"Hey, Chanel, how you doing?"

She acted like I wasn't even sitting here. "What are you doing tonight? I would love to get together."

I rolled my eyes.

"You know, I think it's very unattractive for a woman to see another woman sitting with a man and offers him company when he clearly has some already."

She looked at me, smiled, and gave me a fake ass wave. "Ain't she just your worker or something?"

I was offended and this bitch was asking for a molly whoop in the eye. "I'm not a helper, however, you seem to be, though. You help him bust a nut and you don't see him again after that."

Domo put his hand up, hiding his grin.

"You're going to let her talk to me like that, Dominic?"

"You were rude, and I would like to continue my dinner. I guess I will call you tomorrow or something."

She stormed off and went to join some people at a table. She watched us the rest of the evening. We had a good time and he told me he hated to part ways. I said bye and I went home wishing I wasn't alone. I wanted his fine ass in my bed, but I knew I wasn't ready for shit like that. I would probably fuck around and catch feelings and be one of his bitches looking silly like the bitch from earlier.

Chapter 3

"Open the fucking door, bitch."

I had only been in my place for two months now and somehow Drew had tracked me down. I hoped that Peaches didn't tell him because I would be so disappointed in her. I didn't know what to do. He was kicking a banging on my door and I was so scared of what he would do if he got in.

"Get out of here, Drew, before I call the police."

He got so angry by me saying that he banged harder. "You know I would cut your throat if you ever threatened me with the police again. Now open the door I just want to talk."

He must have lost his fucking mind. I ran to get my phone and called the one person I knew would help. Domo. Maybe he could call him and tell him to leave.

"Hey, I thought you would enjoy the day off."

I screamed when I heard the door explode and hit the wall. He had gotten in. "Please help me. Drew is here and he's going to kill me."

Before Domo could answer, Drew had me by the neck. He grabbed the phone and slapped me across the bed. I balled into the fetal position as he rained blow after blow.

"I just wanted to fucking talk to you!" he yelled, punching me in the back of the head. I started to feel dizzy.

"Get out! Why can't you just leave me alone, Drew?"

He started laughing. "I told you this was my pussy and I wasn't letting you leave unless you were in a body bag."

I knew it. This was the day I would die. He unbuckled his pants and pried my legs open. I couldn't believe he was about to violate me again. He gripped my thighs so tight it felt like he was pulling the skin off. He roughly shoved his dick inside me and it hurt so bad because I wasn't wet.

"Yeah, you miss this dick, don't you?" He pushed my legs up and was roughly fucking me.

I was pounding his back with my fist and he slapped me across the face. I just stopped fighting him and let him do what he wanted. He was fucking his heart out and I just lay there. He came deep inside me and I had never felt so disgusting in my life.

"Get your shit. You leaving and coming home where you belong," he ordered.

He pulled his pants up and opened my drawers throwing clothes at me.

"I'm...I'm not going anywhere with you. I don't love you anymore and I can't take you doing the things you do to me. I'm begging you, just leave."

He turned around and ran up and wrapped his hands around my throat. "Bitch, you better tell me you love me and that you're coming home. Say it!"

I couldn't say anything since he was choking the life out of me. I started to lose consciousness when he suddenly let go.

"Nigga, move and watch you get a third eye. Get the fuck up."

I was so relieved to hear Domo's voice.

"Nigga, I don't know who you are, but you got the wrong nigga. This my bitch and this is none of your business," Drew said, looking down at me without an ounce of fear in his eyes.

"You know me and if you want to keep knowing me you're gonna leave her the fuck alone for good."

He slowly turned his head and was shocked at who had a gun on him. "Domo? Nigga, what the fuck you doing in my girl house, nigga?"

He put his gun away. "I don't think I'm gonna need the strap for this one since I got your attention. Now if you value our business and your life forget about her and act like she never existed. You know what the fuck I can do."

Drew backed down and I couldn't believe this monster, this woman beater, this rapist motherfucker just turned into a complete bitch. He threw his hands up and backed out the room, blew me a kiss, and left.

"Bella, you ok?" Domo came down and pulled me into his arms.

I was in a lot of pain and I knew my face was swollen from the blows Drew delivered. "Yes, I don't know how he found me, Domo. He's never going to leave me alone no matter what he tells you."

"Shhh, it's ok. He knows me and he knows I don't make idle threats. You good?"

I tried to sit up but fell back because I was still light-headed. "How did you get my address? I didn't get a chance to give it to you," I questioned him.

"I pulled the paperwork you filled out for me," he said, pulling out his phone and unlocking it.

"You should have killed him," I said, looking at him feeling Drew's cum seeping out of me.

"My father taught me a long time ago to never mix

pleasure with business. I'm sorry but he brings me a lot of money, but I won't let him hurt you again. Just trust that."

I hated those words. Money always trumped bitches and I guess Domo was no exception to the rule. "Yeah, I know: money over bitches, right? He rapes me and he gets to just walk away. Thank you for coming, though." I was able to stand and the pain between my legs made me buckle.

"It's not that, Bella. I still have business to do and I just can't let what you and Drew have going on step in the middle of that. If you were my woman than it would be something different. Not that you're not important enough it's just…Look I'll protect you and I can start by getting you out of here. I can send some people to get whatever you want to keep."

Where the hell did, he think I was going? He had been good to me these past few months, but I couldn't put my trust in him. Money is his motive and I can get butt fucked by a group of niggas but as long as he supplying them, he won't touch them. He was right, though. He ain't owe me shit and I had to remember that I was alone in this world besides my father and maybe Peaches. I had to make sure she didn't sell me out before I put her in the category.

"Where am I supposed to be going?" I asked with an attitude. He peeped and looked me dead in the eye.

"Look, don't get mad at me because I ain't the nigga that did you like that. I tried to give you some play and you shut me the fuck down. I don't have time for games. Either you fucking with me the long way or we just a boss and worker, you feel me? I got nothing but respect for you, but you need to put that anger in the right place, sweetheart."

I wiped the tears from my face because I told myself after this shit, I would never shed another tear after today.

I would never let another man bring me down to this level and I would only depend on me. I could accept help from Domo, but I wouldn't depend on it. He was just like every other nigga in my eyes and I wasn't about to get snake charmed again so from now on it was me, myself, and I.

"Can you wait for me to take a shower so I can scrub the blood and cum from between my legs?" I said sarcastically.

He stopped looking at his phone and looked at me. "Do you want to go to the hospital?"

I shook my head. "I just want to take a shower and get the hell out of here."

He put his phone to his ear and walked out the room. I grabbed some clothes and a fresh towel and went to scrub myself of the filth that was coming out of me. I couldn't even begin to scrub hard enough. I tried to singe the skin off my pussy so I would have any trace of him on my body. I got out and put my clothes on. I stopped to look in the mirror and saw the marks on my neck from where he strangled me. I had a busted lip and the whole right side of my face was swollen. I knew what I had to do. I had to get something to protect myself. I had to get me a gun and learn how to shoot it. I would be ready the next time he came for me.

I got left the bathroom and I could hear Domo on the phone. I eavesdropped and tried not to even breathe to hard so he couldn't hear me.

"I know, Pops, but I can't let her go out like that. You gotta see what he did to her...I know but fuck him. We got plenty of money coming in and I could pick up a new nigga like it was shit with what we got...Aight, but if the nigga come sniffing back around her it's going to be an issue."

I crept into my room and held my chest: he does

care. Why did he put on that front? I guess he had to act hard at all times. I heard his footsteps and I acted like I was looking for something.

"My peoples coming through. Let's go."

I didn't ask any questions as I said goodbye to my first apartment. I was so proud of it and now I had to give up because Drew found out where the hell I stay. That reminded me, I had to call Ms. Peaches. I pulled out my phone and went to her contact.

"Hey, Bella, boo."

I rolled my eyes, prejudging before I could even ask her anything. "Hey. So, Drew came over and whooped my ass. You got any idea how he knew where the hell I lived?" I asked with much attitude.

"Bitch, bye. You know the fuck I ain't give him no info on your ass. How the fuck you even come at me like that Bella?"

I felt bad and I believed her. She always kept it one hundred, so I played it off. "Girl, I know you didn't say shit. I just wanted you to know what happened." I hoped she bought it because I didn't want to lose our friendship.

"Now tell me what happened."

I didn't want to get into it while with Domo because I wanted to talk to her about him too. "I will holla at you later, ok?"

She said ok and hung up.

"So, you ain't what to talk because I was right here, huh?"

Is this nigga psychic. How the hell did he know that? "Wrong. I heard her man in the background and I got nervous," I lied.

I rubbed my neck trying to relive some of the soreness. I knew it would be stiff in the morning. I already had the ritual down packed since it happened numerous times. All I needed was a box of Epsom salt and a hot towel.

"Can we stop at the store?" I asked Domo.

He was being very quiet and after working with him for three months he was never this quiet. "I can get you whatever you need. I just want you to get some rest. I know you think I'm a fucked-up nigga, but I had to learn the hard way about other people's problems, and I know it's not good for my line of work. Trust me when I say I don't want to see you hurt and I won't ever let you get hurt again."

I leaned over, even in pain, and kissed him on the cheek. I don't know why but I felt like he deserved that. He doesn't know I heard his conversation or that I knew he really wanted to fuck Drew up.

"What was that for?" he said with a slight grin.

"You're a good man and I'm glad to have you around even if it's just a 'worker and boss relationship,'" I said, making my voice deep like his.

He laughed and tapped my leg. If this man can make me smile even after what just happened, any woman in the world would be lucky to have him.

We pulled up on Washington directly in front of the beach. It was a white building that looked like an original structure from when Miami started to first build up. It was beautiful. Dom came over to my side and scooped me up out of the car, carrying me like you would a baby. I melted in his strong arms and he didn't even struggle when he used one hand to put the code in the gate. He carried me up the short flight to the front door and put me down. When he opened the door, my mouth dropped. It was absolutely gorgeous. When you first walk in the entire hallway had blue and white marble floors. The bannister to the steps was gold and I don't have time to explain the furniture and setup. The kitchen was gourmet and I was surprised to see a little Hispanic woman cooking when I walked in.

"Mr. Birkdale, I made lunch just in case," she said smiling at him and me.

"Thanks, Satia. This is my friend, Bella. I believe she is originally from your country."

She smiled and walked up, giving me a hug. It was warm and inviting. "You're Dominican?" she asked preparing two plates.

"Yes, my father is Dominican, and my mother was Puerto Rican."

"They made such a beautiful young lady." She was trying to be nice, I guess. I knew my face was fucked up from the hurting Drew put on it earlier.

"Thank you. Umm, where is the bathroom?"

Domo pointed to the hallway. I went to the bathroom and put some cold water on my face. I stared in the mirror telling myself that I wouldn't fall for this man. He had a woman, he had a few, as a matter of fact, and I didn't want to join his harem. He always had women coming in and out of the office and I always had the displeasure of hearing him dick them down. His main was Ja'Tori, the girl who he was fucking on my first day, and the bitch was a real piece of work. Not good enough for him, if you ask me. She was mean as a snake and very high maintenance. I was sending jewelry and all kinds of Louboutin's to her whenever she got mad at him. I was never that kind of girl. Yes, I loved not to be broke but I never dared to be a spoiled ass woman. I looked at myself in the mirror once more and left out the bathroom.

"Girl, you missing out on some good food. Satia can throw down."

I went to the table and saw she had made some

chicken and spinach paninis and beans. Domo was right too: that shit was off the hook. It reminded me of when my mother was alive.

"I want you to stay here until I can get you in a place of your own," he said, biting into his sandwich.

I watched him chew and I was drawn into to even that was sexy. His dark skin was flawless, and he had a five o'clock shadow that was nice and neat. The waves on the top of his head waved at me every time I saw him. He was a bad motherfucker.

"Is this your house? I mean I don't want to interrupt your life any more than I already have."

He wiped his mouth with the napkin. "You not interrupting me. I enjoy chilling with you so now I get to chill with you all the time. Seems like a bonus to me."

I started to pant a little because everything he said seemed to be perfect. "Ok, well, I still need some stuff from the store."

He nodded and we finished eating.

Satia showed me to a large beautifully decorated room upstairs. It was presidential as shit and I fell into the king size bed and sunk in. The jacuzzi had steps leading up to it and it say off the floor. The dressers were Victorian style and there was even an adjoining bathroom. I was on love.

"I see you like the room."

I jumped when I heard his voice. "You scared the shit out of me, boy. Yes, it's amazing, Domo."

"I'm glad you like it. I'm going to run out and grab your stuff and the guys will be here with your clothes soon. I got them to take your furniture to my storage warehouse. They also have your computer and stuff so you all set, mamí."

I got up and hugged me and he wrapped me up tightly. "Thanks for all of this. You treated me better than a man I been with damn near my whole life, Domo."

I could hear him inhaling my scent and I closed my eyes. I didn't even realize we were stuck in that same position until I heard a woman clear her throat. We broke apart and saw Ja'Tori standing there with her arms folded.

"What's all this, Dominic?"

I walked over and sat on the bed, kind of relishing the fact she was so upset. He could do better than a spoiled ass grown woman.

"I have a houseguest. That's all you need to know."

She looked at me then him. "You must have lost your mind if you think this bitch is going to be sleeping here with you."

I saw the anger in his face when she referred to me as a bitch. "Don't disrespect her because she hasn't disrespected you. Now go in the room and I will be back in a minute. I have to get some shit from the store."

She looked at me, gritted, and walked away. Domo winked and left, closing my door behind him. It was slightly uncomfortable that I was in here with her because she clearly didn't approve and 30 minutes later, she came to let me know just that. She opened the door without even knocking.

"You think your real slick, huh? Feeding him some sob story about how you needed his help and he came running. Oh yeah, I was on the phone with him you called. That's my man, honey, and you need to tell him you don't want to stay here before I have to move you myself." This bitch thought I was a punk bitch apparently. She had that shit all wrong. "First of all: Domo wants me here. He brought me to his house and told me I could stay until he found me a place. Yes, honey, until HE found me a place. Funny: you don't live here, but I do. Did he ask you? I didn't think so. Now what you're going to do is move your ass outside that door frame before I go the fuck off and crack your ass in the mouth."

She was steaming. "This shit ain't over, bitch. Watch me work." She left the room and I started laughing at her.

Silly rabbit.

Domo came back and had the stuff I asked for. He didn't miss a thing. He got me some Dove body wash but I didn't ask for it.

"That's my favorite scent on a woman. I would like to have it lingering in the office."

I smacked my lips and waved him off. "Your woman came in here telling me I needed to leave."

He shook his head, cracking a smile. "This is my house and you can live here as long as you want. She all talk, so don't trip on her."

I looked at him with my mouth turned up to say I wasn't. "I already know. That's your boo, though."

He licked his lips with a cute grin on his face. "Ok, so I'm guess I will see you later. I'm about to run around."

I was kind of sad he was leaving. I was scared to be alone. I stayed in the room all night watching TV and reading a book on my tablet. I heard Domo come back in that night. He went straight into his room. I was able to fall asleep after taking some extra strength Tylenol and drinking two glasses of wine.

The next morning, I woke up to the smell of sausage and my stomach started to growl. I got up, brushed my teeth, and washed my face. I wanted Domo to know I woke up like this. I left out my room and hurried to the kitchen. If Satia's breakfast was like her food yesterday I was ready to get down. I rounded the corner and was surprised that it was Domo cooking. He was flipping an omelet and I caught his eye when he came in. He had on an apron and he smiled as he wiped his hands on the apron.

"I gave Satia the day off. I usually don't show women my cooking skills so soon, but since you're just my friend you get it right away."

I looked over the island counter and saw he had home fries, toast, and muffins. I was impressed. Men don't usually do this. I noticed he had three plates. He pushed the omelet onto the plate and went and took them to the table. He waved for me to come sit down. I moved quickly because it looked so good. He placed ketchup, jelly, and butter on the table. I picked up the orange juice and poured some into my flute. This was nice and since I was starving, I dug in. My throat was still very sore, so I had to slow down. He can cook his ass off. Domo had joined me now and we chatted a little bit. I grabbed a muffin and cut it, smearing butter inside. I heard the heels clacking and I knew Ja'Tori was coming. When she came in the dining room, she wore a look of disgust.

"I didn't realize we were having guest for breakfast," she said, cutting her eyes at me and placing a napkin in her lap.

"Since this is my house that makes you a guest too, don't it? Cut the shit, Ja'Tori."

I kept eating and kind of laughed at her little shit talking keeps backfiring.

"If you don't feel like going in today that's fine."

I waved my hand off at him. "I'm fine. I've had worse days after him." Which was true.

"Ok. Well, it's seven and since the car is at your old spot you can ride with me."

Ja'Tori slammed her cup down and got up, storming out of the room.

"Wow. You need to go handle that," I said, biting into my eggs.

He kept eating. "Nah, she good. I just spent a lot of time on this and I'm a big dude. I gotta eat," he said cutting his omelet and taking a bite. He was just so cool and nonchalant about everything. It was good to see a man who didn't blow up at every instance.

"Thanks for breakfast. I'm going to go get ready."

I got up and headed to my room. When I hit the corner, I could see Domo watching me walk out. I felt tingles down to my pussy and I had to play with my clit while in the shower so I could get this horny sensation off. I decided to wear a pair of high-waisted shorts and a crop top. I had to fix my face up and cover my marks, so I did my makeup and made sure I was beat for the gawds and threw on my accessories. I was ready and looking damn good. I slid into my sandals, grabbed my clutch, and headed for the door. When I got downstairs, Domo was sitting on the couch reading something on his phone. He must have felt my presence because he turned around and looked blown away.

"Seems like you ready then." He got up and opened the door for me.

"Thanks," I said, heading out the door.

Ja'Tori came walking down the steps and she took one look at me and rolled her eyes. "Doesn't look very professional," she said as she pushed the gate hard and went to her car.

That bitch had one more time and I was going to get loose on her stupid ass. She got in the car but didn't leave. That's not until Domo opened the door for me and I cutely slid into his car. She skirted off' over was dramatic as shit. I mean thinking of it from her side, yes, I would be a little jealous too. The ride to work was quiet and Domo couldn't keep his eyes off my thighs. I knew I was thicker than a Snicker and was used to the glares of men and the jealousy of women. I had my mother's shape and I loved it. I could wear anything and looked like a video model or better.

"Keep them eyes over there," I said, messing with him.

He cleared his throat and pulled up to the valet. "Girl, you knew what you were doing when you put that on."

I blushed and went to open my door, but he grabbed my arm and I jumped. "It's ok. I just wanted you to wait until it's opened for you. You're a lady."

He was melting my heart. I wished that I wasn't so damaged because then I could take all of it as a compliment and not a ploy to get me to trust him so he could whoop on me and degrade me like Drew did. He was sweet just like Domo and then he turned into his true form. I couldn't assume every man was the same, but I was scared to be right.

We walked in the building and a woman sitting there with her hands on her hips, tapping her foot. I continued to the elevator as Domo went over to speak with her. She was a new one because I hadn't seen her before. I got on the elevator and Domo and the woman ran up and jumped on. She had her arms wrapped around his waist and was trying to kiss him. When he looked over at me, he stopped her. She was clearly embarrassed that he didn't accept her kiss and she turned around, waiting for us to get to the office floor. When it opened, she stomped off and waited for him to open the door. When we got in, I sat at my desk as they went in the office. The phone rung and when I went to answer it was none other than Ja'Tori.

"Put him off the phone."

I decided to be funny. "Well, Mr. Birkdale is indisposed at the time. Would you like to leave a message?" I could hear her smack her teeth in the phone.

"Put him on the phone, now!" she yelled into the phone. I can bet he didn't answer his cell that's why she called the office.

"You know what? Sure."

I hit the speaker and told him he had a call. I looked at the phone to see that the line was still flashing. I went on to start my job and got to writing up contracts. He was a busy ass dude. I don't see where he finds the time to be a boss nigga in the streets and boss nigga in the office. I commended him.

The day's end finally came, and I was more than ready to get the hell in the bed. We had meetings and shit all day and I was all worked out. Domo came out the office and I got up and grabbed my things.

"You hungry?" Damn all he wanted to do was eat.

"Yes, we stayed two hours late. Now it's dinner time and you better be getting something good," I said, walking out behind him.

I don't know why but I had a question that needed to be answered. I stopped before leaving the completely out the door and turned to him. "Why do you have so many women? I mean Ja'Tori apparently thinks it's just her, so why?"

He put on a smirk. "Ja'Tori is a good woman. Sometimes. We aren't officially a couple, so it's not cheating. I have so many because I can't seem to find the one that would make me drop my life to go rescue her in the time of need, the type of woman who wants nothing but to be respected, and not what's in my pockets, the type who would accept a job because she wants to have her own instead of jumping to the next nigga with money. "You know anybody like that?"

My pussy started throbbing for some reason. He was talking about me — I knew he was. I put my head down in shame because I was nobody's prize. Look at what I allowed to happen. He raised my chin up and he surprised me when he kissed me on my lips. I couldn't help it. I let him kiss me even after I thought he was fucking that girl in his office. I still let him rub on my ass. We were so close I could feel his dick fill with blood and travel down my stomach. He must have been huge. I heard the elevator and I pulled back to see a lady from another office getting on.

"Stop. I'm sorry, Domo. I just don't think I'm ready for anything right now. I mean look what happened yesterday. I'm scared that, this is my life."

"I'm not him, Bella. Stop treating me like I am."

He brushed past me and hit the call button for the elevator. I quietly walked to him and just stood there looking like a fool.

"Are you still feeding me?"

He laughed and wrapped his arm around my shoulder. "I'm always gonna feed you if you hungry, mamí."

We had a nice dinner at Hot Off the Grill and it was amazing. I felt like we were on a date. I never had that. Drew never took me anywhere except to his friends' parties or their houses and I hated it because every time it would end up with me fucked up for being friendly. This was nice even though we weren't dating. I could tell the chemistry had changed a little. A man can only take so much rejection. When we were leaving, he got a call that pissed him off and he threw money on the table and stormed out. We had a few drinks, so I was tipsy and tried my best to keep up with him. This time he didn't open my side of the door. He just got in and I hopped in right after. He didn't even wait for me to close the door before he pulled off. Something must have been really wrong. I saw him pass the exit to his house and he kept driving until we got to Liberty City. I been here a few times with Drew, but I usually don't set foot here. I watched the dope heads shuffle across the street, almost getting hit by cars. I didn't dare ask him what we were doing here because after being a drug dealer's woman for so long I knew not to ask questions. We pulled up in front of a pink house with brown shingles around it. I could see a child covered in filth sitting out front. She had to be about eight and she looked so pitiful. Domo got out of the car slamming the door so hard I couldn't believe it didn't shatter. He walked up to the girl and grabbed her hand and led her into the house.

I sat in the car for about ten minutes and I got pissed off. This wasn't a neighborhood that I should just sit in and I was about to call myself a taxi. I didn't know what Domo was doing but people kept stopping and looking into his car and I was about to go before they robbed my ass. I went to my phone's browser and put in taxis in my area. I was startled by a chair coming through the front window of the house I sat in front of. I rolled the window down so I could hear what the fuck was going on.

"Get the fuck off me, you pipe headed bitch. This why you wanted to keep her? Look at my fucking sister," I could hear Domo yelling.

Shit was about to get real. I saw the door swing open and he emerged with the little girl. A black woman came running out behind him pounding him in his back. He kept walking and he opened the back door and told the girl to get in.

"Dominic, I am still your mother. You need to respect me. Now give mama some money until I get my check. I'm sick Dominic."

He laughed as he walked around the car to get into the driver's side. She pounded and beat on his car and he peeled out. I didn't need to know what the hell happened until he said something.

"This is my sister, Marion. That was my mother and I got a call that she was getting high while my sister sat outside starving and dirty."

I didn't say anything. It was none of my business to speak on it.

"This your new girlfriend? She real pretty," she said snickering.

The poor baby didn't even know she was being mistreated. She was still smiling. I thought about the child I lost and how I would have been the best mother I could be. We arrived home and we walked in the door; Domo took Marion upstairs. I could hear him running bath water. I went to my room and closed and locked the door. I didn't know what kind of mood he was in, but it damn sure wasn't good. I could hear the doorbell and I wasn't even curious to who it was. I turned on the TV and I started to hear arguing. I went to the door and I heard none other than Ja'Tori.

"Well, what the fuck you want me to do with her?" I heard her say.

"I said watch her until I get back. What the fuck you think I want you to do? I need to get her some stuff so she can go to my aunt's house tomorrow," Domo barked at her.

"Why don't you ask your little roommate, huh? I'm

sure she looking for brownie points by now."

I peeked my head out and I saw a familiar look in his eyes. One that told me she was about to get her ass whooped real bad. He didn't touch her though.

"You know what? This shit ain't gonna work for me. I need a real woman, not some spoiled little bitch who can't even look after her nigga little sister while he makes a store run. Get out. I sure will ask my roommate because I bet, she won't blink twice because she a real woman. GET THE FUCK OUT AND DON'T LOOK YOUR RAGGEDY ASS BACK!"

I closed my door and got on the bed like I wasn't listening. I could hear the alarm chime telling me somebody just left. Domo ended up asking me to look after Marion until he came back and I put her in the bed with me. She was a sweet little girl and when she fell asleep, I wouldn't let Domo pick her up. I let her sleep with me. I was tired myself and I took more Tylenol because I was still hurting, and I went to sleep.

Chapter 4

The next day, Domo told me I had to hold the office down for a whole month and I didn't know why. I couldn't do whatever the hell he did, and I was afraid to do so. When he told me he was going to Georgia to drop off his sister and he was going on a trip, I got pissed. He expected me to just live in his house and run the construction company alone? I didn't know what the hell I was doing. He left telling me I had it and he trusted me. What part of the game was this? The first week was boring as hell. He called and checked on me a few times, but that was about it. He would text me "good morning" every day, but it was at like three a.m. He must have been somewhere with a way different time zone. He also texted me good night. I kind of missed him too. I wondered what he was doing.

By the third week, I had started to talk to Peaches every day because I didn't want to feel as lonely as I was. We made plans to chill tonight and I was so excited. I had healed up nice and my face was cleared up. I picked a nice tight-fitting maxi dress and my new favorite pair of red bottoms. I made sure I was bad as shit before I stepped out on the porch and watched all the people hustle and bustle up Washington. I got some catcalls and it was nice for my self-esteem. I decided to drive the Porsche; Domo welcomed me to all his vehicles so that's the one I wanted. I revved her up and watched heads turn. I felt like a boss in this bad boy. I started driving over to Peaches and Bizzy's place. I was scared that I might run into Drew, but if Peaches hurried her ass up, we could get the fuck out of here. I texted her phone and she emerged quickly. She ran up to the car and slid her hand across the top admiring the expensive vehicle.

"Daaaaam, bitch. Domo being real good to you, huh?" she said looking around in the car.

"Girl, you know it ain't like that. He just helping me out." I didn't tell her about us kissing and shit because I knew she would hype me up about it.

"Yeah, ok. You staying in his shit too. I know y'all gonna be fucking soon. Won't you just give the boy a chance? He might be your husband, bitch."

I laughed and I started to feel sick. I pulled over and as soon as I opened the door I threw up. "Damn, bitch. You was already drinking?" she said, rubbing my back.

"No, I been throwing up for the last few days. I think I ate something that got me hurt."

"You not pregnant, are you?"

I couldn't be. I hadn't had sex and then it dawned on me. "Drew took it from me when he showed up to my place. I couldn't be, though…right?" I said looking at her with hopeful eyes.

"Go to the CVS, we gonna find out."

We went and picked up a pregnancy test. I asked the associate could I use the bathroom and she let me. Peaches stood outside while I pissed on the stick. When the results came, I threw the stick and wailed. Peaches must have heard me and started banging on the door. I opened it and when she saw my face she knew.

"Oh my God. What are you going to do?" I didn't want to have an abortion, but I knew who's baby it was and I couldn't take having it, having to be around him.

"I don't know, Peaches. I can't have a baby with him."

Needless to say our night was ruined. We went back to Domo's and just chilled and smoked some trees. I couldn't keep his child. I would never be done with him and I didn't want to put the baby in harm's way. I went to bed feeling totally fucked.

***

A few days later, I was in the bubble bath thinking of ways to abort without feeling shitty. I had to because there was no way I was going to carry another child for that nigga. I just had to do what I had to do. I heard the door chime and assumed it was Satia coming in for the day. We had gotten close. She said Domo takes trips like this all the time and it had something to do with business. She also told me I was stupid for not snatching Domo up and that he deserved a nice girl like me. I had made a decision that I was going to get him and if it didn't work than I would just move on. Life was short and I deserved a little happiness. Thinking of Domo made me horny and I decided to relieve some stress and slid my finger down into my pussy and worked it. I thought of our kiss and his dick growing and I exploded. I heard a light tap on the door and quickly got myself together.

"Come in, Satia." I was a woman and so was she, so I wasn't embarrassed about her seeing me in the bathtub.

"I see you all ready for me."

I jumped and tried to gather bubbles to cover myself. "I thought you were Satia," I said as Domo stood there not even trying to hide the fact, he was staring at me. I decided to make it fun and stood up, grabbed my towel and walked up to the mirror and started drying off.

"Shit! You about to get more than these flowers girl," he said, pulling a bundle of roses from behind his back. "I just wanted to say thank you for holding it down for me and I was sorry about not opening the door for you when we left dinner. Yeah, I remember little shit like that."

I walked up and gave him a big kiss on the lips. I don't know what got into me, but I was hot and horny. He looked surprised as I placed my hand on his dick and felt it rock up.

"Are you sure?" he asked.

I bit my bottom lip and dropped my towel. That shit drove him crazy and he pulled me to him and shoved his tongue in my mouth. Fuck this. I wanted to be happy and I just had to take a chance.

"I'm sure. I been thinking about us."

He started kissing my neck and if felt good my eyes rolled in the back of my head. "Ok, what about us?" He scooped me up and laid me on my bed. Rubbing his hand over my naked body. I wasn't sure he wanted me to answer now.

"I was..." I was stopped when I felt his tongue on my clit. I clenched the sheets and he stopped licking.

"Tell me." He went back and slurped and sucked my pussy and I knew I had to be cross-eyed by now.

"I want you...OHHH MY GOD!"

He squeezed my thighs as he tongued my pussy like he was licking an ice cream cone and he seemed to be enjoying doing the shit. "I wanted you since I saw you in the liquor store," he said between licks.

I couldn't hold it and I exploded all in his face and tried to catch my breath. He wasn't letting that happen.

Before I knew I had lost all my air when he slid that pole into my wetness. I clinched his back and held on for dear life.

"Shit, this pussy is gold. Finish telling me what you want." He thrust in and out and I couldn't take the dick, but I was trying.

"I want you, Domo! I want to be yours!"

He was sucking my nipple and I came again. "You wanna be my bitch?"

My mouth was wide open, and I was still having an orgasm. "Yes, I want to be your bitch, Domo."

"That's right. Whose pussy I'm in?" he grunted.

"Yours, baby, she all yours. I'm cumming. Fuck!"

I was cramping from that last orgasm. He flipped over with his dick still inside me and put me on top. He gripped my ass and bounced me on his dick, and it was driving me insane. This is what I was missing out on. I was a damn fool. He smacked my ass and tried his best to bust me wide open. He let go of my ass and grabbed my titties and put both nipples in his mouth.

"Shit, you got a nigga ready to bust all in this shit." I didn't want it to be over, so I hopped off and got in a doggy style position.

He grabbed my hair and dove in. He leaned down in my ear. "You know, I saw when you first went into my office. I watched the whole thing and I wanted to give you this dick, but I didn't want to scare you off."

That made me even wetter. He watched me and it gave me goose bumps. It made me cum again and this time he came with me. We lay on the bed and looked into each other's eyes.

"What made you change your mind, Bella?" he said after kissing me.

"I don't know. Everybody is vouching for you and I just wanted to see where it goes. You know your fleet of hoes gotta go, right?"

Before he could answer there was banging on the door. Without an invite it flew open and Ja'Tori was standing there like she had seen the devil himself.

"Oh, yea, motherfucker? You disappear and now I find you fucking this hoe?"

I got up ass naked and all.

"Mr. Birkdale, I tried to tell her you were busy," Satia said, running in.

"Nah, no apologies, Satia. Can you make me and my new bae some lunch? What you want to eat, baby?" he looked at me.

Ja'Tori charged me and I hit her ass with a one hitta and knocked her the fuck out.

"I told you it was over. Now out of respect I'm not gonna clown you but, I need you to leave before I get nasty."

She got off the floor and looked at me like she was deciding whether to try again. She chose wisely and left.

"Come back over here," he said just as calm as ever.
I slid back under the covers and as soon as our bodies touched it was on again. We finally took a break and went to eat whatever Satia cooked. She was smiling and grinning as she placed our plates on the table.

"I have something to tell you, Domo, and I hope this doesn't affect us," I said putting my fork down. He kept eating so I guess I was just going to blurt it out.

"When Drew — you know did what he did to me — apparently, he got me pregnant."

He dropped his fork and looked at me. "Are you keeping it?"

I immediately shook my head.

"Ok, then there's no problem."

I was relieved he didn't get mad. I mean, how could he? It's not like I fucked him willingly. After breakfast, I made an appointment to go to the clinic. I hit Peaches and asked her to roll with me because it wasn't Domo's responsibility to do it. We sent Satia home and finished exploring each other. Hell, what am I saying? We fucked like rabbits until we passed out.

***

The morning had come and gone, and Domo had moves to make and it made me sad that we couldn't keep eating each other up. I didn't know what I was getting into, but I had a feeling I would soon find out.

"You wanna just roll with me? I gotta be honest; I'm collecting from Drew today so if you wanna stay here that's cool," he said sliding into his fresh pair of KD's.

"I mean as long as you with me I'm good, babe."

He came down and kissed me and smacked my butt. "Ok, well hurry up. I know how long women take to get dressed."

I got dressed and we were out the door. I was kind of nervous, but I knew that Domo had me. We pulled up to a nice house and Domo opened the door to let me out. He spun me around, looking at me.

"I can't wait to get you back home," he said as we walked to the door. He opened it and I saw all of the guys that Drew ran with and some he didn't. When they saw me with Domo they looked at Drew and he looked like the blood left his face.

"Aight, we got a little bit of time to make this shit happen. I got a surprise for my baby and I don't want to keep her waiting," he said, kissing my cheek.

The looks on their faces were priceless. I felt the tension and decided to just go have a seat.

"Nah, boo. This our money, baby, we collect this shit together."

Drew stood up and threw his bag at my feet.

Domo didn't like that shit at all. "See, nigga, I was trying to be nice by not blowing your fucking brains out for that bullshit you pulled at her spot. But since she mine's now you need to know I won't hesitate to peel your shit back and dump your motherfuckin' ass if you ever disrespect her again. You hear me, nigga?"

"Yeah, aight. This my last drop then, nigga. Ain't no loyalty in this shit and I been dealing with you for years."

Domo shook his head. "Check this shit out, nigga. You think it's cool for your so called' woman? You a cold bitch for that one. And as far as your last drop? You right — this is it. Good luck finding this good raw for my prices now get the fuck outta here. By the way, she was pregnant and she pulling that plug so go weep, nigga!"

I was more than surprised and embarrassed. I know it was truth, but he just jumped me all the way out there. "Domo, it's ok. You didn't have to say all that."

He looked at me like I just disrespected him or some shit. "When I'm talking, baby girl, don't interrupt me. Pisses me the fuck off." I got frightened because he never spoke to me like that. Were these some early warning signs?

Drew looked at me with hate in his eyes. "You better not kill my fucking baby, bitch."   Before I knew it Domo cracked him in the head with his gun. "Didn't I fuckin tell you not to disrespect my woman, nigga?" He kept beating him. "Drag this nigga outta here," he told the other dudes.

Bizzy was his friend so I could tell that pissed him off. After the shit settled I sat there quietly as he spoke to all of them. He made a call and a woman showed up and grabbed all the bags and loaded them into her car.

"Who is that?" I asked Domo when we were getting in the car.

"She one of my loyals. She was working with my father now she works for me. Look, I got a certain level of respect on these streets. I can't let my woman dictate what I should and shouldn't say. That's how niggas lose respect in the game: when they look soft. I'm sorry if that hurt you, but you said you wanted me and you gotta know the rules to this shit."

I guess he could be right. "Ok, Domo," I said quietly as we pulled off.

"Don't say it like that, Bella. I won't ever hit you or treat you anything less than the queen you are." He reached to stroke my face and I jumped. He pulled over and threw the car in park.

"Bella, look at me." I couldn't because I was ashamed of the fact, I couldn't allow him to make a movement without flinching. "Bella, look at me!" he screamed, and I put my head up to look him in the face. "I'm sorry about everything that happened to you. You're in good hands, though, mamí, and I'm going to try my best to make you forget about that nigga and whatever he put you through. I been knew about all that shit. When y'all would come to parties and you had black eyes and bruises on your arms I knew. I thought, 'how could he treat somebody so beautiful and sweet like a dog?' I never could wrap my mind around that shit. Don't worry about anything. From now on I just wanna make you smile."

I knew I promised I wouldn't shed any more tears,

but they just flowed. "I just don't want to die, Domo. How do I know you won't turn on me?"

He came an inch from my face and started kissing my tears away. "Because I said so."

All I had was his word. He pulled off and we got to a dealership. I know he didn't need any more cars than he already had.

"Dag, you trying to open a dealership yourself?" I said, unbuckling my seatbelt. I got used to him opening the doors for me I just waited for him to walk around and do so.

"It's not for me; it's for you."

My jaw dropped as I looked at all the luxury sports cars. "Are you serious?"

He gave me an I should know already look. "Pick one. Matter of fact, pick two."

I ran around the dealership sitting in different cars and I felt like a true boss's wife. He watched me like a kid in the candy store. When I finished running myself around, I picked a Lamborghini that I was getting custom painted pink and a Bugatti that I wanted custom painted candy apple red. They said they would deliver them when they were complete.

"I can't believe you," I said, trying to hide my smile.

"Well believe it because it only gets better from now on."

I lay back on the headrest and enjoyed the ride. I actually felt something I hadn't felt in a while.

Happy.

Chapter 5

"Awwww, how you feel, boo?" Peaches asked as we left the clinic.

I had my abortion and I was in so much pain. It was God's way of telling me I was wrong.

"Yeah, I'm good. I guess once I get my medicine I can be relieved."

"Ok, well lets go fill it and we can go to your house and get lit." She was my homie for real. She was always there for me no matter what.

While waiting for my prescription this irritating bitch kept walking past me looking. What the fuck was her problem? Before I could ask her Peaches was on it.

"You got a fucking problem, bitch?"

The girl mean mugged us and walked to the front. We both looked at each other and shrugged the bitch off. When we were leaving we saw her standing at Peaches car like she was waiting on us.

"I want to know how long you been fucking my man?" she directed towards me.

"And who the fuck is your man?" I asked, getting ready to whoop this bitch's ass if she popped off. I was in pain but I can still beat a hoe's ass.

"Drew, bitch. Don't act stupid."

Me and Peaches looked at each other and bust out

laughing. "Sweetie, you need to update your agenda book. I don't want that piece of shit no more than you want that black eye he gave you on your face," I said noticing she tried to cover her eye with makeup.

"Bitch, don't worry about what the fuck we got going on. He said you tricked him into getting pregnant."

He was a lying ass nigga and these bitches fell for his bullshit. "Chile, bye. I got better shit to do than to argue with a stupid stalker bitch. By the way, it helps if you use concealer because you ain't hiding shit with that cheap ass foundation." I moved her out the way of the door and got in. I saw the sadness in her eyes and it was all too familiar.

"That hoe just don't know, huh?"

I shook my head no and watched her in the rear view mirror. I'm glad I got out.

When we got back home, I saw Domo's car and wondered what he was doing home. I went in and Peaches went straight to the kitchen and grabbed two glasses so we could pour up. I went upstairs and didn't see Domo anywhere. He must have been in the basement. I walked down and when I could to the bottom I heard muffled moans. This nigga better not be fucking some bitch. I grabbed the closet stick like thing I could find so I could beat they ass if he was. I went and cracked the door and I saw a naked man on the floor bloody and gagged. There was plastic covering the floor and Domo had 2x4 with nails in it. It was covered with blood and flesh. One of Domo's men, Lando, started pouring rubbing alcohol on the dude and he rolled all over the floor trying to scream out.

"You think it was worth it, muthafucka?" Domo smacked him again with the stick in the face and ripped off some of his skin.

I was horrified. I went back upstairs quietly so he

wouldn't hear me. When I got to the kitchen, Peaches was already drinking. I grabbed the glass and started guzzling it down.

"Slow down, your ass gonna be sick as shit."

I didn't tell her what I saw downstairs. I didn't know he could be capable of that type of shit. He looked so scary. I turned to grab the bottle and knocked it on the floor scaring myself.

"Bella, that's you, babe?" I heard Domo yell up the steps.

"Umm...yeah. I dropped something."

"Ok, give me a few minutes and I'm coming up," he yelled and closed the door. When he did come up he had no shirt on.

"Wassup, sexy." He kissed me on the check.

"Hey, baby. What you doing downstairs?" I questioned like I didn't know.

"Just bagging some trash, babe. What y'all drinking?"

Peaches looked at him and took the rest of her drink back. "Some Jose Cuervo." She was looking at his chest and it was making me a little mad.

"Aight, Peaches. I'ma holla at you tomorrow." I said.

She downed another glass and gave me a hug. She gave Domo one too and I could have sworn I saw her squeeze. Maybe I was tripping, but I wasn't feeling that shit at all.

"I wanted to ask you what you thought about me opening a strip club? I need some more clean businesses because money coming fast, and I need it to look legit."

I wasn't too comfortable with that but it was his money so he could do what he wanted. "It's cool with me as long as you ain't fucking none of them bitches."

IN LOVE WITH THE CONNECT

He smacked my ass and kissed me on the neck. He almost made me forget what was happening earlier in the basement.

"I just wanted to let you know I saw you. I just didn't want Peaches in your business."

He looked at me with confusion. I guess he caught on after I diverted my eyes to the basement. "It's business. He stole something from me and I don't like taking loses. That's all you need to know," he said walking away and disappearing upstairs.

I saw movement out the back window and I saw Lando walking with a large suitcase out the back gate. I knew that man's body was in there. I went up behind him and told him about what happened today. He was upset because he felt like Drew just didn't get the message well. After seeing what he can do I knew he was no joke and Drew was about to get fucked up if he didn't fall back and I can't say I wouldn't be grateful.

***

After a few months, I finally was able to somewhat put the images out of my head of the man in the basement. I wonder what he took from him. He never told me but I can bet it was money. Domo was still being good to me but he had a little mean streak. It was like his behavior was erratic and he had to catch himself. He always apologized and gave me gifts when he would blow up. I think I'm falling in love with him and I hoped he fell the same. I know it seemed early, but his presence does things to me that had never been achieved by any man. I wanted to tell him I loved him so bad but I didn't want to look like a jackass if he didn't feel the same way. I felt like there wasn't anything he wouldn't do for me and felt the same way. He was on power moves and I wanted to be there with him the whole way. He was going to run Miami one day and I wanted to be the queen on that nigga throne.

It was Saturday and the grand opening of our strip club. I handpicked some of the girls and Domo picked the rest. They were talented girls and had "give me that money" asses. I was in the office with Domo when Diamond came in. She had on a G-string and a skimpy bra.

"I wanted to know if I could be moved to spot one. I think since I headlined in King of Diamonds, I might be the main attraction. These bitches can't do it like this." This bitch had the nerve to turn around and start clapping her ass.

"Hoe, what the fuck you think you doing? I know the fuck you see me standing here. My nigga ain't no customer. You need to focus on them."

She rolled her eyes and looked at Domo leaning over the desk in his direction.

"Yeah, go tell the DJ" He grabbed my thigh and gripped it. "Babe, you gotta chill. Wasn't no need to snap on the girl. She was just trying to show us what she got."

I narrowed my eyes at him. "Yeah, ok, nigga. She a fucking hoe and the moment my back turned she gonna make her move."

He pulled me on his lap. "I don't see nobody but you, Bella."

We kissed and another interruption came in. It was Louis, the bouncer. "Aye, it's nine. Time to let them in, right?"

I looked at my phone and nodded. "Let's do this, baby," I said getting off his lap.

He got up behind me and we went to the floor. The niggas was flooding in and it was packed. I watched Domo circulate and talk to some people. All the niggas looked like ballers and I knew we was about to make a killing tonight. I went to the bar and had a few shots. I watched Diamond on stage twerking and clapping her ass. They were throwing hundreds and fifties at that bitch. She was getting coin and I got jealous when I saw Domo watching her. She got offstage and pulled him up. She wrapped her legs around his neck and pumped his face to her pussy. This bitch had me fucked up. She really thought she was slick, huh. I went to the stage and grabbed her by the hair and started wailing on her ass. Domo snatched me off her and carried me to the office while I was kicking and trying to get back to that bitch. He dropped me on the office chair and put his hands on the back of his head and stared a hole through me.

"You must be fucking crazy, Bella. You attack a bitch on the opening night!"

I stood up and walked up on him. "You had your face all in that bitch pussy and that was disrespectful to me. You act like you didn't know I was here."

He kicked the chair over, and I got scared. He walked up to me and I fell and balled up ready to take some blows. When I didn't feel him hit my I looked up and he was looking down at me like he was confused.

"Oh my God. Bella, get up. What the hell has that man done to you?" I was still scared to stand but he came down and picked me up. "I'm not gonna hit you, shawty. That shit breaks my heart when you get ready for me to put my hands on you. I'm not him. Still that was real fucked up what you did out there. If you can't control yourself, you need to stay home. Matter of fact go head home. I can get a ride. Take the car."

He handed me the keys and I left. I know I made us look bad and I felt like shit for it. I just think that bitch need to know her place. She on some snake shit and I know it. I was pissed driving home. I don't see how he couldn't have seen it the way I did. I got home and threw my shoes down the hall and headed upstairs. I grabbed a bag of trees, a sheet, and rolled me a jay. I smoked and ordered some pizza. I was lonely as shit and I looked at the clock and it was now two o'clock. Where the hell was Domo? I called his phone and it went straight to voicemail. What the fuck? I texted him and he never hit me back. I was heated and I was ready to go look for his ass. I stayed in the bed watching my phone and it never lit up. I dozed off and even as the light hit my eyes, I could feel the emptiness in the bed. I got up and ran downstairs and Domo was nowhere in sight. I went back upstairs and called his phone and it still when to voice mail. I started getting worried and I called hospitals to see if he was there. I called the police to make sure he wasn't locked up. He better has a good excuse because I was pissed. It was now seven a.m. and I sat in my room crying my eyes out. I heard the door chime and I tried to get myself together. He walked in the room with a bundle of roses.

"Where the hell were you? Fucking that bitch, Diamond, from the club?" I said through sniffles.

"Man, no. I fell asleep at the club. I was drinking and fell asleep in the office." He went and started to take off his clothes and he went in the bathroom and turned on the shower.

"You think I'm slow, huh? You slept at the club, nigga? You need to jump straight in the shower when you come in?"

He got in and ignored me. I know the fuck he ain't think I was dumb. "Stop being insecure. You know ain't none of these bitches got shit on you."

I got on the bed and put my face in my hands. Something wasn't right and I knew it. There was no way what he told me was true.

He came out and lay on top of me. "Baby, you know I ain't giving your dick to nobody."   He kissed the back of my neck and sent those pussy throbs that only he could deliver. He ripped my underwear off and shoved his fingers inside me. I gasped as he worked my pussy and I juiced down his fingers. He slurped my juices off like butter from a biscuit.

"I wouldn't give this pussy up for shit, girl."

He kissed it and tongued it until I was raining down on his face. He got up and went to the bathroom and washed his face. He came back and lay down next to me.

"Damn, I can't get no dick, huh?"

He kissed my forehead. "You gotta earn it back after showing your ass last night."

I smacked my teeth and we lay up together. While I was I snuggled up to Domo he told me he didn't want me to work anymore. That just wouldn't do. I don't want to be some stay-at-home bitch who does nothing now that I found the freedom I been desiring.

"I don't want to stay home, baby. I thought you wanted a broad who does for herself?" I said, lying on his chest watching TV.

"Who said you were staying home? I want you to open a business. I need clean money babe and since you with me, you with me," he said, picking up his phone checking the message that just came through. When he opened it he immediately closed it and put it down.

"Who was that? You didn't seem to want to hear from them."

He flared his nostrils like I said something wrong. "It

was broad I use to fuck sending me tittie pics." He was so honest it hurt.

"Well did you tell her you have somebody?" I asked.

"Yeah, I told her that before me and you started our shit. She ain't hearing it."

I couldn't stand a bitch who couldn't get it through her head. "Well you want me to call her?"

He shook his head. "Ain't nobody to worry yourself over."

I didn't like his answer. Why the fuck couldn't I check the bitch? "Aight, but she gonna be hurt if she come at my nigga," I said with a slight attitude.

"Don't act like that. I'm here with you, ain't I?" I nodded just like the passive bitch I was.   I felt like he wasn't telling me the whole truth. He got up and went into the bathroom and I debated whether or not I should go in his phone. I hit the home button and it was a password on it. Dammit. I walked over to the bathroom door and knock.

"Hold up, bae. Gimme a sec." I could hear him sniffing really hard. He came out with a white substance on his nose.

"Babe, was you just snorting that shit?"

His eyes were glossy and he looked zoned. "Is it a problem if I was? You wanna try it?"

I never did any of that shit. I knew people who did, like Peaches and even Drew, but I never fucked with it. It was a hot drug of choice in Miami. I never got with it.

"Nah, it's not for me."

He went to the sink and chopped up a line. "Just try it, Bella. It's good shit."

I went to the glass mirror and took the rolled dollar bill and sniffed the line up. It burned like hell and I immediately felt the euphoria. He took some and put it on his tongue and shoved it in my mouth. It got numb right away. We kissed and for some reason every touch felt better than before. I was in a zone and I didn't want leave it for shit. He carried me to the bed and bent me over and inserted his tongue in my ass. He held my ass cheeks apart and ate the groceries. He stopped and got under me and pulled me onto his face. I rode it and came countless times until I couldn't anymore. His dick was nice and ready. I spit on the tip and tried to go down as far as I could but he was so big I gagged easily. I went up and down on it until he gripped my hair pulling me up.

"Shit, you almost made me cum. Get in position."

I knew that meant get into doggy style. I felt something being slid around my neck. I grabbed for it and Domo smacked my hand away.

"What is this?"

He pushed my shins back. "Pull your feet down and don't let go."

I did as I was told and he slid his dick in me and I bit down on my bottom lip. He pulled tighter on my neck as he pumped in and out of me. I was in heaven. He made the pain my pleasure and took me to a new height. He bit my ass cheeks and smacked it until it was numb. I started cumming so hard I almost chocked myself to death.

"Tell me what you want, Bella." He was digging my guts out.

"I want the dick, daddy."

He pulled his dick out my pussy and worked it into my ass. I screamed out in pain and he yanked the belt harder. He was ripping me apart. Once the pain eased up it turned into bliss. He flipped me over and pushed my legs back as far as they could go. He shoved it back in my ass and after ten minutes of violent strokes he came and he pulled it out slowly.

"Damn, babe, I might have to marry your ass."

I was laid on the bed all fucked out. Everything seemed to be going slow around me. Domo's phone ringing brought me back to reality. He was in the bathroom washing up. The number wasn't saved so I grabbed my phone and tried to enter it but it hung up already. It went off again and this time Domo came out to answer it. He picked it up and ended the call. He thought fucking me was going to make me forget his ass didn't come home.

I tried to be as normal as possible, but I the fact I thought he was cheating on me was driving me crazy. He would take calls and walk downstairs, or he would get texts and wouldn't answer them. I walked in the room the other day and he locked his phone and put it under his pillow. I prayed to God he ain't doing shit, but my inner bitch told me he was. I didn't even know what I would do. One night I answered his phone while he was in the bathroom and the bitch hung up. I knew it was a female because only bitches do weak as shit like that. My father used to cheat on my mother and she never left him. He was so good to her and you wouldn't even think she felt any type of way about it. She used to tell me sometimes you have to accept certain things to be comfortable. I took that as he could fuck who he wanted as long as she was number one and was getting anything her heart desired. She told me that every man cheat and that I better get used to it because it's going to happen. I didn't want that type of life, though. I wanted my husband to want me and only me. He was on some suspect shit and I was going to find out what the fuck was going on.

Chapter 6

Three months later

The strip club was doing so well that Domo hired a temporary replacement to run the construction company. I was so mad because he would be spending all his time in a fucking hoe house with a bunch of bitches. Tonight, he thought I would be staying home but I asked Peaches to come with me to the club so I could see what the hell was going on down there. I wanted to surprise Domo so I got a new dress and a new pair of stilettos so I could look bomb. I snorted a bump off my hand after I was completely ready. I had started using coke more often and it wasn't bad as I thought. I wasn't addicted; I just liked the high. I even sprinkled the shit on my trees before I rolled it. Peaches got to the house looking like a certified dime piece. Even after kids her stomach was flat, and she had shape for days.

"Look what I got." She pulled out a sack of tree and a baggie of coke.

I clapped my hands in excitement. She made a line for us on the living room table and we sniffed it up. We rolled a Woodie and got high as hell. We got into her Lexus and headed for the club. It was after twelve, so I know the shit was popping off. We parked in the owner's spot next to Domo's car. When we got to the line we walked straight in since the bouncers knew who I was. The place was packed, and the strippers were in full swing. I looked around for Domo but didn't see him.

"Let's get a drink, bitch." I wanted to find him, but a shot would be cool.

"Let me get two shots of Patron, Rick," I yelled to the bartender.

I downed mines and waited for the next round. When he dropped them, I threw it back and told Peaches I was going to find my nigga. When I got to the office the door was locked. Since I got the key, I unlocked it and walked in. I was stopped dead in my tracks when I saw Diamond up on the desk and Domo between her legs fucking the shit out of her. She saw me and smiled. I ran over and punched him in the back of the head and started beating her ass. She tried to cover her face, but I was beating the dog shit out of her. I turned to him and he had his face in his hands.

"Look at me, Domo!" I screamed at him.

He stood up and tried to hug me and I pushed him with all my might. "Babe, I'm sorry; I swear this shit wasn't nothing."

Diamond stumbled to the couch. "What you mean it 'wasn't nothing'? I'm pregnant with your fucking baby, nigga."

I was hoping I heard her wrong. "This bitch pregnant, Domo? Why the fuck would you do that to me? I guess this the bitch that was sending you titties and shit, huh?"

I was crying so hard my stomach hurt. I couldn't believe I believed all his bullshit. He was a snake motherfucker and I was done with niggas.

"I didn't mean to hurt you, Bella. You know I want you to be my wife."

I started laughing. This nigga must have been high as fuck. "Marry this hoe. It's over, Domo. I can't let you start doing me wrong too then it will never stop." I turned and kicked Diamond in the face, and she started gushing. I walked out and I could hear him screaming my name.

Fuck him.

***

After filling Peaches in on everything she seemed more disappointed than I was.

"I'm sorry, Bella. Where you wanna go?" I wished like hell I didn't let him move me out of my place.

"I don't know. Just take me to the house so I can get my clothes."

When I got home, I ran upstairs and packed as many suitcases as I could. I didn't want Domo coming in trying to change my mind. How could he do this to me? He knows what the fuck I been through. The bitch having his baby at that. I thought we were good. I cried as I threw the suitcases to the bottom of the stairs.

I went to the front door and I saw Domo pull up. I grabbed the bags and tried to carry them, but they were heavy as shit. I struggle to get them down the steps.

"Where you going? Don't leave. Just talk to me," he said, trying to take one of them out of my hand.

I let it go and kept walking. "You can keep that one. I can buy new clothes," I said, trying to walk around him.

"You really gonna let that bitch come between us?" I threw the bag down and looked him dead in the eye.

"You let that bitch come between us. You made me look like a damn fool and I'm tired of y'all niggas treating me like shit. Fuck you. I'm done with niggas." I picked my bag up and tried to leave but the gate wouldn't open.

"I can't let you just leave me. I fucked up but I swear

I can make it right. Just come back inside."

It's a trap just like with Drew. "Bye, Domo. Please, just open the gate for me."

He came up and came down to kiss me. I turned my head.

"Come in the house, now. I'm not going to say it again." He grabbed my bags and took them back in the house.

I was so scared at this point because I didn't know what he was about to do. I took some terrible ass whippings and I was prepared for the worse. I went into the living room where he sat looking frustrated.

"I know you fucked up right now. It wasn't supposed to be that way babe. The shit happened and I just couldn't stop."

He was cutting me like a knife. "I wasn't good enough for you? You fed me your bullshit and you turned out just as I thought. I can't stay with you because it's never going to end. I just want to go."

He got up and ran up the steps and I heard drawers and shit. I thought about just sprinting and trying to hop the gate, but it was tall as shit and I knew I wouldn't make it.

He came downstairs with his bag. "Well, you must be taking me with you then."

He was dead serious. "I don't have time for your mind games. You're having a baby with another bitch. You made me love you and you just shit on me."

"You love me? Why didn't you tell me?"

"Does it really matter now? You got who you want. Go start your family."

I thought about the back gate. I broke for the back door and he grabbed into a bear hug. "I love you too Bella.

I fucked up and let my dick think for me and I'm sorry. Just let me make this up to you baby."

I tried to wiggle free and he wouldn't let me go. "Put me the fuck down I hate you, Domo." I was kicking my feet trying to get down.

"No, if you leave, we both leaving."

He took me outside still fighting to get loose. He put my seatbelt on he and told me I better not move. He went and locked the door and came back to the car. He drove off and I just sat in the seat, defeated. He pulled out his phone and I saw him go to a contact and he called it.

"Yeah, get it ready like now." He waited for the other person's response. "Yea, Brazil. Rio De Janeiro"

I just looked ahead as we drove into Miami international terminal. "What the hell are we doing here?" I said still being as stubborn as a mule.

"We going away. You said you wanted to leave so were leaving."

He unbuckled my seat belt and got out. When he opened the car door, I was sitting there with my arms folded. He scooped me out the car and put me on the ground. "Stop it. Let's go and if you still don't want to be with me by the time, we come back I will leave you alone forever."

I nodded like the submissive punk I was. He put me down and we walked into the airport with nothing but the clothes on our back. We went to a counter that read private flights.

"Yes, Mr. Birkdale. My jet should already be on the runway."

I didn't even know he owned one. They escorted us to a gate, and we walked into the terminal and my anger subsided for the moment when I got onto the plane. It was some "lifestyle of the rich and famous" type shit. It was woodgrain everywhere. It had a full bar and a living room type setup. There was a huge TV and a bedroom in the back. This shit was amazing.

I looked at Domo and got pissed all over again. "You think whisking me away is going to get me to say 'oh he cheated and got a bitch pregnant. Oh well'?"

He pulled me to him and kissed my neck. I could smell that bitch's pussy on him and pushed him away.

"You still smell like that bitch. Get the fuck away from me, Domo."

I went to the room and closed the door behind me. I heard dinging and the pilot said it was take off. I didn't go back out and I could feel the plane moving real fast and then it was like I was upside down. I could see out the bedroom window we were in the air. After a minute we were steady; I could hear water running and I guessed that Domo was showering. The door opened and Domo was standing there with a towel on. I couldn't help but glare. I caught myself and just stared out the window. I could hear him going in the closet. I couldn't believe he had clothes and shit already on here. That must be in case he needed to leave in a hurry. The turbulence scared me because it felt like we were about to crash. I jumped, and Domo must have noticed because he got in the bed and grabbed me from behind.

"Just leave me alone. You only sorry because I caught you, Domo."

He started kissing my neck and I felt myself responding to him. I thought about how he was fucking her, and it brought tears to my eyes. "Let me make you feel good, baby."

He reached under my dress and started fingering my

pussy. I tightened my thighs and he got up over top of me and pried my legs apart. He dove face first into my pussy. I was powerless to stop him once he was working magic on my clit. My toes were curling, and I was gripping the back of his head as I came in his mouth. I felt the head of his dick pushing inside and gasped while he long stroked me.

"I'm sorry, baby. I won't ever hurt you again," he whispered in my ear after we were done and laying in our sweat and cum.

"How do I know that? It hasn't even been that long, and you already did me dirty as shit," I said, angry at myself that I let him fuck me.

"I got you, Bella. Let's just start over, babe. I promise I will fire her, and you won't ever see her again."

I forgave Drew for worse. Maybe we could just try again. He was good to me and I know it might seem dumb, but I believed him. I was still very crushed. "So, what about the baby? Is she going to keep it?"

He exhaled heavily and sat up. "She said she don't want to, but she won't make an appointment for the clinic."

That bitch! "This is all your fault. You couldn't just make me happy? Damn, what is about me that keep making y'all niggas do me like this?" I got up and went to the window, looking out. I couldn't see shit but clouds.

"You didn't do shit, baby. I was just a dumb ass nigga. I got you, though. You believe me?"

I nodded. I didn't know what to believe. I was probably making a big mistake and deep down, I knew it.

I fell asleep after chewing his ass out for four hours. I got my point across but I still felt like it was déjà vu. I was thinking back to the first time I caught Drew cheating. It didn't play out in my favor at all when I caught him. He didn't even show the slightest bit of remorse.

***

I was out with my father. We were over my aunt and uncle's house. I was checking my phone to see if Drew had hit me back. Usually whenever I was out, he would blow my phone up. I finally got sick of waiting and told my dad I was heading home. When I got there, I saw a car that I didn't recognize in the driveway. I walked in and I immediately knew somebody was fucking when I heard the loud screams. I ran upstairs and burst in my room to find him fucking a bitch in our bed.

"You son of a bitch!" I screamed and started punching him all over.

He elbowed me in the mouth and I went falling to the floor. "Don't you ever put your fucking hand on me again, bitch. Get the fuck outta here before I break your fucking jaw, bitch." I got up and attacked him again and he kicked me backward in the stomach and came over and started wailing on me.

"Since you don't want to leave stay and watch." He grabbed me around my neck and sat me on the bed. "Move and I'ma kill your ass in here," he said I was frozen.

He went down and started eating the girl's pussy and all I could do was watch. He fucked her and was mocking me, talking shit to me the whole time. I never felt so stupid in my life. He started to regularly bring the bitch over there and fuck her while I sat downstairs. I left once and he found me over Peaches house and dragged me back home. I couldn't leave the house for two months because of how he fucked me up.

***

Here I was ready to let this man off the hook just like I did so many times with Drew. What was I doing? I saw Domo start to stir and I got up to go pee. When I looked out the window I saw ground. We must have been at our destination. I went and woke Domo up and told him we had to get seated. The seatbelt sign had come on. We landed and if felt like the damn plane was crashing. Domo laughed at my facial expression and I couldn't help but bust out laughing. We left the plane and it was very festive even at the airport. There were drums and people dancing. Domo grabbed my hand and we headed to the transportation. We caught a cabbie to a beautiful house on a hill.

"Whose house is this?" I asked taking in the beauty of my surroundings.

"It's mines. I brought it a few years ago when I visited here."

We walked up to the door and when he opened it I was in awe. He had the house looking like a magazine for extravagant homes.

"This is amazing, Domo."

He wrapped his arms around me from behind. "Anything for you, girl."

"I hope you mean that."

He crossed his heart and even licked his finger and lifted it to the sky. "I won't fuck up like that again. I love you, Bella."

I turned to him. "I love you, too, Domo."

I didn't have any clothes, so we had to go shopping. When we went into the garage of the house there were three cars: a Maserati, a Camaro, and a Jaguar. We chose the Maserati and we zoomed off. We drove down the thin streets like we lived there forever. I was having so much fun from the car ride I was screaming while I laughed. We arrived a shopping mall. It had some nice ass clothes. I picked up everything I saw. The shit was high as hell too. I went to look at bathing suits and I grabbed a few bikinis. I had to buy shoes to match everything and we basically spent the whole day getting our wardrobes up.

After getting cleaned up and dressed cute we went to a Brazilian grill and Domo got the singers to sing for me. I was blushing the whole time. He didn't take his eyes off of me. He was really trying to win my ass over, and he was pulling out all stops. After dinner we went to a party in a large warehouse. It was off the hook. The music was live, and people were dancing around and having fun. We decided to join in, and I was swinging my hair trying to keep up with the other women. Domo was just grinding on me as I danced. He slipped off and I saw him talking to a guy and he handed him something. I kept dancing like I didn't see shit. He came back over and pulled me to the bathroom. He pulled out a baggie of White Girl and we snorted a few lines. We were high as a kite and we floated back onto the dance floor. I had to admit; this was the most fun I had in a long time. He was keeping his promise to make me feel better. That bitch wasn't getting all of this and that somehow put my mind at ease. I made myself believe she was only a fuck and that he loved me.

We sat at the bar drinking some shit I couldn't even pronounce. This beautiful woman walked up and whispered something in Domo's ear. I thought I was about to have to get locked up in Rio, but Domo nodded and she walked up to me.

"You're very beautiful. I saw you dancing, and I wanted to ask if you would join me? I asked your husband first and he said it was okay."

I shrugged and we went on to the dance floor. She got behind me and placed her hand on my stomach and raised my hands in the air and slowly stroked her hand down my arm all the way to my ass. She moved her hips and I moved with her. I could feel her lips brushing against my neck. I didn't know if it was the drugs, but I got a rush from her body touching mines and her titties were rubbing against my back. I never been into girl, but this had me feeling some type of way. Domo watched us as we danced. I saw the lust in his eyes. When the song was done, I walked back over and sat down with Domo. I didn't know she was still behind me until she placed her hand on my back.

"What else do you guys have planned for tonight?"

Domo shrugged his shoulders.

"Nothing really," I said, taking another shot. That shit burned the hell out of my chest.

"We can go hang and I can show you guys some hot night spots. Follow me to my house and I can drop my bike off and ride with you. Let me grab my purse from the back."

I didn't think much of it, but when she walked away Domo grabbed my waist and whispered in my ear, "Stop being so green. I got a strap in the car just in case this bitch trying to set us up."

I didn't think about that. He may have been drunk, but he was on point. She came back with a purse and said she was ready. We followed her on her motorcycle to a cute little house sitting on a steep winding hill.

"You guys can come in if you want. I just need to grab some things."

Domo went under his seat and grabbed his gun; he came around, let me out and tucked it into his pants. When we entered it was pretty average? Nobody was there so I assumed she stayed here alone.

"Your English is good. Where did you learn?" called to her in the back."

She came out with a bottle of tequila and some shot glasses. "We learn in the schools here. You look like you belong here. Are you Brazilian?"

I took my glass and shook my head. "I'm Puerto Rican and Dominican."

She raised he glass to us and we took our shots back. "Well it's a nice mix. You're very sexy. I'm Leri anna, by the way." She filled our glasses up again and we threw the shots back.

"I'm Bella and this is Domo," I said, pointing at him.

She went and turned on her radio.

"I thought you were taking us somewhere," I said as she started to wine to the music.   Domo was looking at her like he wanted to fuck the shit out of her. She was sexy and I couldn't deny it. She danced over to me and grabbed my ass and start dancing on me. I looked at Domo and I could tell that he was turned on. If this was what it took for him not to stray again then he could have it. I started touching on her like she was doing me and that must have got her turned on because she stuck her hands between my legs. Domo noticed and he came to me and started kissing me. He was rubbing her ass. She went to unzip his fly and she pulled his dick out and she started to go to work on it. He was loving the shit. I can't believe we were doing this. I just caught him cheating on me and now we having a fucking threesome with some random bitch.

"Can I taste it?" she said, looking at Domo as she rubbed my pussy.

He nodded and she raised my leg and pushed her face into my pussy. She was killing it and I was loving her ass right now. Domo ass sucking on my titties and touching all over me and it made me feel so out of it, I came in her mouth. I had her hair gripped and she was still sucking my clit. Her tongue was thick, and she stiffened it to fuck my pussy hole. She was jiggling my ass while she tortured my already sensitive pussy. She stopped and started sucking Domo's dick again. He was nice and hard. He sat on the couch and she crawled over to him and started sucking and licking his balls. I didn't want to feel left out, so I went and started sucking his dick. He pulled out his coke and snorted some. He put more on his hand and put it in front of me and I sniffed it off. He pulled her up and she put her finger up telling him to wait and she came back with a condom. He pulled it out and ran it down on his dick with her mouth. I watched her straddle him and she had the same reaction to his dick as I'm sure most girls would. He waved his hand to me and I sat next to him and he started kissing me while she rode his dick. I wasn't jealous or even mad. I guess it felt good to me too, so it didn't matter.

"Fuck get up. Let my baby get some dick."

He pulled the condom off and he turned me over and started fucking me from the back. He was busting me wide open. I saw Leri anna get under me and she was licking my clit and his balls, going back and forth between us. I started cumming and I saw her hold her mouth open and caught all of it in her mouth. Domo pulled out and nutted all on her face. He kissed me and smacked my ass.

"You guys are a lot of fun. Too bad you don't live here, huh?" I heard her say while I was gathering my clothes.

Boom! Boom!

I jumped and turned around to see where that loud noise had come from. My ears were ringing. I saw Lerri anna laid on the floor with blood coming from her chest and mouth.

"OH MY GOD! What did you do?"

Domo pulled his jeans up and tucked the gun into his pants. "Nobody will ever fuck my wife and live to tell it but me."

I was in total shock. I sat on the couch and Domo had to dress me. He pulled me out the door and I stumbled as I looked back and saw her lifeless body lying on the floor.

"Are you fucking crazy?" He smiled and shook his head.

"I'm not crazy, but I'm crazy when it comes to you. I know I fucked that hoe and broke your Heart, but I couldn't deal with knowing somebody touched you and enjoyed my pussy. Wouldn't you kill for me, Bella?"

In an idiotic twisted way, I attempted to make sense of it. If he would kill somebody for me then he must love me. We rode back to the house and we fucked in the jacuzzi and he told me over and over how much he loved me, and he wanted me to be his wife. He also said I wouldn't have to worry about Diamond fucking up our life together and he would talk to her when we got back.

***

We had been here three days so far and we did something special every day and today was no exception. Today we were on a yacht cruising with no destination. I must have been more fucked up than I thought though; he cheated and killed a bitch in less than forty-eight hours and here I was bunned up with him on a fucking yacht, drinking champagne and relaxing with him. He said he had one more surprise for me when we got off the water. He took me to a small church, and he told the pastor he wanted to marry me. He pulled out a huge diamond ring and slid it on my finger.

"Are you serious? Where the hell did you get a ring from?" I said looking at it then him.

"I ordered it from the jewelry store we passed yesterday. I paid them top dollar to rush it for today. I told you I wanted you to be my wife. I know your pain still fresh, but trust me, baby, when I say you will never feel that pain again. Just marry me, Bella."

I was trying hard to go over it in my head. We hadn't been together a whole year and after the shit I been seeing, I didn't know. I just blurted out yes. They performed a ceremony and told us we could file the certificate and they would give us a certified copy.

"We really got married!" I squealed, kissing him all over his face.

"I know this isn't the wedding of your dreams, but we can work on that later. I had to make you 'Mrs. Birkdale' before you tried to leave me, girl. I want you locked in on us. Just promise me you won't let no bitch come between us. Matter of fact don't let shit come between us. You my queen, girl." He kissed me nose and then kissed me.

"I promise."

We went back to the house and consummated our marriage. We took pictures and I posted them on Facebook and put "Mr. and Mrs. Birkdale" as the caption. We got flooded with likes and love buttons and the "congrats" comments started coming in. I saw a comment from a person I didn't recognize at first. It said, "congrats, stepmommy." Then a sonogram picture popped up. I clicked the profile and it was Diamond. That bitch was stalking me and shit.

"This bitch, Diamond, just put a sonogram picture on my Facebook."

I gave him the phone and he looked pissed off. "Fuck that bitch, Bella, she just trying to ruin your day, babe."

I blocked her and we continued our trip. What was going to happen if she didn't have an abortion? I didn't want that reminder in my life forever. I hoped he could talk some sense into that bitch. I was enjoying Rio but after almost two weeks of being out here I was ready to go home. I guess he was right about what he said. I wouldn't want to leave him by the time we got back. I was even more in love with him if anything. He made me so easily forget things that should have been a big deal, like him killing Lerri anna right after we fucked her. He was doing something to me, and I didn't know what. It was like he wanted me to be familiar and normalize myself with that type of behavior. I didn't know if I should fear that or not. He would protect me. I knew he would.

Chapter 7

When we got back home, I was still on cloud nine from the trip. It was the best time I ever had in my life and I wanted more of it. I had forgiven him, and we were moving on from the bullshit. He introduced me into his world and I fell right in. He told me about the trips he takes and that it was moving weight. He stays for long periods, so he won't be noticed. He said the next time he went I could go with him. He wanted me to open a day spa in my name so it could be used as a front. Of course, I agreed. I named it Queen of Kings day spa. I worked with the contractors and got it just the way I wanted it and we opened as soon as the paint dried. I hired a staff of eight masseuses, two tanning specialists, a front desk receptionist, and a barista for the café. We charged top dollar and all the women who started to come in were connected to niggas in the game. I felt good having my own business and I felt like shit was finally on track. I had a new husband and a completely new life. I told him to sell the strip club as soon as he could break even for it. I didn't want to have to wonder about shit else with his ass.

I sat in my office looking over the sales for the month when I heard a loud ghetto ass voice getting closer to my door. I knew exactly who it was, and she came bursting in smiling.

"Peaches, what I tell you about being loud in my damn building? People come here to relax not here you screaming ass running through the hall."

She sat down in the seat in front of me. "Well your little assistant act like she ain't want to let a bitch by so I had to let her know who the fuck I was again."

I shook my head. She was a damn fool.

"So, look, I'm having lil' Bizzy's birthday party at my house and I wanted you and Domo to come by."

I loved her kids so of course I was coming. "Ok, cool. What you need me to bring?"

She waved me off. "Nothing but your gifts and that fat ass."

"Dyke ass. Anyway, what time should we come through?" I pushed the papers back in the folder and looked at my phone to check the time.

"It's Saturday at one."

I stood up grabbing my purse. "Ok, cool. Let's get something to eat, bitch. I'm hungry as shit."

Peaches stood up and I noticed she had a bruise on her arm. "Damn, what the fuck happened to you?"

She covered it with her hand. "Ain't shit, fell going up the steps."

I looked at her with a knowing face because I knew she was lying. "Bitch stop lying. Did Bizzy hit you?" She looked away.

"We just got into some shit, is all. He good, though. He knows I will shoot his ass again."

"No, it's not cool. Come on, Peaches. What you always tell me?" I said, referring to when she kept telling me to leave Drew every time, he whooped my ass.

"It's all good. I got this."

I rolled my eyes and we left to go eat. Before we went inside, we blazed up. She offered me some coke, but I declined. I told Domo I didn't want to do the shit anymore. I told him he needed to stop too. I didn't want to get hooked off the shit. He promised he would. We got to the Pollo Empara and grabbed some chicken sandwiches. While we were eating, I saw a car pull up outside the window and thought, *awwww shit*. It was Ja'Tori whack ass.

"That's Domo old thang. I knocked her ass out a minute ago."

Peaches watch her walk in and rolled her eyes.

"Bitch, bye. You know you shitting on that bitch. You got the ring, girl." She was right, fuck that bitch.

"IIi, Bella, I see you slimed your way into a marriage," she said, walking up and looking at my hand.

"Call it what you want. I see you still salty as fuck, huh?" I said drinking my soda.

"Bitch, ain't no salt over here. I had the nigga now I don't. I got better shit to do."   Peaches was getting irritated I could see it in her face.

"If you got better shit to do then do it and get the fuck outta my face." I was ready to pounce on that bitch.

"By the way, I saw Domo walking his baby mother into the woman clinic the other day. They look like a family how he was holding her stomach and walking her in," she said with a smirk on her face.

"What the fuck are you talking about? He don't have no baby mother." He told me Diamond was having an abortion as soon as we got back home, which was four months ago.

"Yea, well he was walking with somebody baby mother than and hugged up on her too."   She walked off and I was devastated. How could he lie to me? I picked up my phone to call him and he answered on the first ring.

"How's my beautiful wife doing?"

I bypassed that bullshit. "Is Diamond still pregnant?"

The line went blank for a minute. "She wouldn't have the abortion, baby. I didn't know how to tell you. I just didn't want you to try to leave me." I felt my heart breaking again.

"You were hugged on the bitch going to doctor appointments and shit. How could you lie to me again, Domo?" Peaches was looking at me with pity.

"I'm sorry, Bella, I couldn't just let her go alone. What kind of father would I be?"

I hit the end button. How could I be so stupid? He called back and I didn't answer.

"I'm going back to work, Peaches. Drive me back, please."

I sat in the car trying not to cry. I was his wife and was supposed to have his first child. Now that was taken away from me.

"Ok, honey, call me if you need me," Peaches said as I exited the car.

I went straight to my office, locked the door, and went crazy. I was pacing and talking to myself and I broke down in the corner and wept. I could hear my phone still ringing off the hook, but I didn't answer it. I turned the lights off and laid on the sofa and sulked. I heard knocking on the door, but I didn't answer.

"Bella, it's me baby. Open the door," Domo said.

I didn't move. I just lay there and let him talk to the door.

"You said no bitch was ever going to come between us, mamí. I love you, girl. Open the door."

I still didn't move. I could hear him start to jiggle the handle more violently.

"Open the fucking door, Bella."

I jumped. I didn't want him to scare the clients, so I got up and opened it.

"What the fuck you want to tell me, huh? You're sorry, right? You promised you wouldn't hurt me again Domo. Why can't you just be honest with me?"

He grabbed me up and broke free. "We married, Bella. You my wife and you always gonna be that. I know you didn't want it to go down this way, but I think we can get past this shit together."

I didn't want to get past it. I didn't want some bitch having my husband's baby. "No, it's not going to work for me Domo. Why don't you just go be with your new family because I can't deal with this shit."

He got pissed and smacked the shit off my desk. "Look, you staying with me through thick and thin. That's what we promised and that's what I meant. You try to run from everything and I'm not letting you. Do you still love me?"

"Yes, but..."

He put his hand over my lips. "Then love me then. Don't worry about nobody but us baby."

I shook my head. He grabbed my arms and yanked me to him. "What the fuck you mean 'no'? I'm trying to be good to you, but you're starting to piss me off, Bella."

"How am I pissing you off? You cheated and now you got a baby on the way. I can't even give you your first child now. Now please let me go you're hurting me."

He turned me loose and I rubbed my arm. "Come on, we're going home."

I couldn't just leave in the middle of the day. I had to

run the place. "I have to stay here until we close."

He grabbed my purse and threw me over his shoulder. I hopped down and snatched my purse. "You doing me just like him, Domo. You're trying to control me and think for me and I can't live that way."

He put his face in his hands like he was frustrated. "I can't be without you, Bella. Just come home with me baby."

I heard the sincerity in his voice. "Why? Obviously, I'm not what you want. You just want to have me."

He slammed the door and I backed into the wall. He came a breath away from my face. "I do want you, I just wanted to fuck her, baby. I swear I don't care about that bitch. I come home to you and I treat you like a queen. I never done for any woman half the shit I done to show you love." He kissed me and it felt good. He went to my neck and started sucking on it.

"I can't keep hurting, Domo."

He was unbuttoning my pants and he had them at my ankles. "I'm trying not to hurt you. I just want you to feel good. Let me make you feel good, baby."

He got down and wiggled his tongue on my lips, then he put his thumb in my ass and bounced me on his tongue and I was trying to find anything I could grip on the wall.

"You can't leave me Bella, I can't even think straight when you hurt and it's my fault." He got up and scooped me up and had my legs straddled and he entered me. I had my arms wrapped around his neck and we were banging against the wall. "I love you Bella. Fuuuuuck," he said, thrusting in and out of me.

"I love you, too, baby!" I said, reaching my climax and held on as he fucked me silly.

He came inside me and I lost my head when I remembered I wasn't on any birth control.

"You didn't pull out." I said, feeling his cum seeping between my thighs.

"I want you to have my baby," he said, watching me and gauging my reaction.

"You just want me pregnant to make me feel better about her being pregnant?" I would look as dumb as Amina Buddafly's ass.

"I don't think that's a good idea right now. I mean we keep going through these motions and I want to be stable. You keep lying to me and I don't know if I could trust you," I said, putting my shoes back on.

"We're having a baby, Bella, because I want kids with my wife. Now come on. I still want you to come home so we can work on starting our family. Don't make me carry you out like a baby."

I smiled and thought about the night he carried me out my apartment. "Please try to be honest with me from now on."

He still picked me up and carried me to the car. "I got you, girl. You can get your car tomorrow or maybe the day after. We got a baby to make."

We went home and we fucked the rest of the day. He came in me every time and I asked myself; why does this whole thing seem so familiar. I was letting him run rapid and I kept forgiving everything he did because I loved him just like I loved Drew. I was naive and weak and I knew it. At least he doesn't hit me.

Chapter 8

It was now Saturday and it was lil' Bizzy's party. Domo couldn't make it because he wanted to go talk to the contractors who were building our new house. He surprised me with it the day after I found out that bitch Diamond was still pregnant. He said he would make it after he had his meeting with them. I went to Wal-Mart and grabbed a few toys and a big gift bag. I headed to Peaches house and when I got there, I knew this bitch was crazy. She had over a thousand balloons all over the front yard and a huge sign that said "Anthony's Super Dope Party." That was lil' Bizzy's real name. I walked in and it was so many kids and people I got dizzy.

"That's my best friend, that's my best friend. Biiiiitch come over here and see my baby lookin' all fresh and shit!" Peaches screamed when she saw me. I sat my bag on the table of gifts and went and kissed lil' Bizzy on the cheek.

"Happy birthday, lil' man."

He wiped the kiss off. "Ugh, that's nasty." He ran off and started to play with the other kids.

"Where your husband at?" she said, handing me a wine cooler.

"He said he might come later. He had to meet with the foreman who's building the house. I see the gang's all here," I said, referring to the people I use to hang around when I was with Drew.

I spoke to some of the girls, but the niggas didn't look my way. I conversed with some of the girls and me and Peaches started to gather everybody to sing "Happy Birthday." After we cut the cake, I saw Asia walk in and Drew was with her and their daughter. *Piece of shit*, I thought to myself.

"Bitch, why you ain't tell me that lowlife was coming?" I said in Peaches ear.

"I didn't know he was. I didn't invite him; Bizzy must have. You see who he with, bitch?"

I nodded and grabbed a slice of cake went into the back before he could see me. I texted Domo to see where he was, and he told me he was on the way. I was relieved. I didn't want to be here by myself with him. I walked out back and watched the kids scarf cake and jump on the moon bounce.

"Hey, Bella, you ain't want to speak?" Drew said.

I had chills because I didn't know what he was up to. "Hi, Drew," I said, moving a few inches away from him.

"I just wanted to say I'm sorry for how our shit went. I been going to counseling. I don't know if you know, but I got locked up for hitting Asia and I been trying to change."

I rolled my eyes and laughed. "Yeah, right. Please don't feed me your bullshit. I had enough of it over the years, Drew."

I tried to walk past him, and he grabbed my arm tightly. "I'm trying to make this shit right, Bella. Just hear me out."

I snatched my arm and looked in to see if I saw Domo anywhere yet. "What is it, Drew?" I folded my arms.

"I mean it, I could have done you way better baby,

you needed me to just love you and I couldn't do that right."

I was having flash backs of all the things he had done over the years and I just couldn't let him suck me into his lies. He always said "sorry." "That's good, Drew. I'm glad you're getting help."

Asia walked out and looked at both of us. "Hi, Bella, heard you got married."

Drew looked at me and then looked at my finger. I saw the scariness he just told me was gone. The rage was there, and I knew he was about to go off. "Bitch, you married that nigga! You killed my fucking baby for him, didn't you?" His eyes were red, and his teeth were gritted.

"Why the fuck you even care, nigga?" Asia said and Drew reared back and slapped the shit out of her.

I ran down the steps and I could see people in the window gathering to see what was going on.

"Come here, Bella! Why wouldn't you marry me, huh?" he said, charging toward me.

"No, leave me alone, Drew. Help me!" I was so scared I fell to the ground.

Drew snatched me by the hair and started beating me in the head. "You wouldn't marry me, bitch, but you marry that muthafucka, huh?" he kicked me in the back, and I balled up so he wouldn't punch me in the face.

"What the fuck are you doin'?" I could hear Peaches yell.

He stopped hitting me for a minute and he elbowed her off and came back to me to continue his assault. "You disloyal ass hoe. I should have overdosed your stupid ass." BAM! He punched me in the side.

POW!

There was one gunshot and I moved my hands to

see what must have been a dream. My father was standing there over top of Drew with a gun in his hand.

"Papa?"

I saw Domo run up and he looked at Drew then at me. He darted over to me and helped me up.

"Baby what the fuck happened?" he said, but I was too stuck on my father being here to answer him.

"Drew came in here and started going crazy," Peaches said.

"Baby girl, are you ok?" My father came up and we hugged for what seemed like forever.
"Domo came to get me. He got me a lawyer a while back and they let me out early."

I looked at Domo and he was still very pissed. He was probably mad he wasn't there to protect me. "Are you ok, Bella?" he asked.

I watched the niggas pick Drew body up and carry him to the shed.

"Aye, you got a problem, my nigga?" Domo said, looking at Bizzy who was looking like he wanted to do something.

Bizzy just helped Peaches into the house.

"Let's get you home. Here, take Bella's car," Domo said, digging in my purse and handing my father the keys.

I had a bad headache and my back was hurting so bad. Domo opened the door and he helped me in the car. We drove off with my dad right behind me.

"What was that about? He just went crazy when he saw you?" Domo asked me.

"Asia told him I got married and he went off. He slapped her too."

He punched the steering wheel. "Man fuck. Shouldn't have let you go alone. I just wanted to surprise you by picking your pops up." He was so sweet. I knew now that he really would do anything for me.

"It's ok, baby. I guess we don't have to worry about him anymore."

He shook his head. "I'm gonna run you a bath when we get home. I wish I could kill that muthafucka again." His pride had got to him.

"I'm fine, baby. It could have been worse. I just have a headache is all."

"It's not fine Bella. I keep breaking my promises to you. I can't protect you from him or even me. I keep hurting you too." I rubbed my hand down the back of his head. He was really beating himself up.

"I love you and that's all that matters. You been more good to me than bad."

He looked at me and came in for a kiss. "I love you too, mamí."

We pulled up and I saw my father pull behind us. I couldn't wait to talk to my father. When we got in the house, I sat on the couch waiting for him to join me. He came over and as soon as he sat down, I laid my head on his shoulder.

"I missed you, Papa. You just don't know what I been through."

He wrapped his arms around my shoulder. Domo went straight upstairs, probably to run my water.

"That's a good man you got on your hands. He's a little rough, but he has been completely honest about everything. Don't get me wrong. I'm more than a little pissed off he cheated on my baby and knocked some whore up, but he owned it and I have to respect a man who puts his cards on the table. Sometimes you have to let a man be a man, though baby, girl. He doesn't love you any less."

I was surprised Domo would tell my father that and I wasn't surprised my father thought it was ok. "Yeah, I'm trying to forgive him. But forget about me. What are you going to do?"

He put his hands up and lay back on the couch. "I don't have to do shit. I got money waiting for me. I'm good. You know I'm pretty pissed off you didn't tell me what that Puto was doing to you, mi Amor? You know I would have sent somebody to kill his ass."

"I don't know, Dad. I just didn't want anybody to die. I was stupid, huh?"

He shook his head. "Not stupid, just scared for your life, baby girl."

He kissed my forehead and we talked a little more until Domo came down. "I got your bath all set for you, Bella," he said, helping me up.

"Where are you going to stay, Papa?" I asked, getting up.

"You know I got connections for days. I told one of my loyal soldiers to hook me up and that's what he did. I got a spot all set up for me. You know your pops ain't no slump nigga girl. Now come give me a kiss."

I kissed him and I heard Domo telling him he had what he needed, and he could pick it up from his spot tomorrow. I hoped Papa wasn't thinking about getting back into his old life. I went upstairs and Domo came in with my iPad. He turned on my Pandora and set the station to a 90's R&B mix. He knew what I liked.

"I told your father he could borrow my car, but he made a call and some nigga popped up like spider man and shit to pick him up."

I laughed because even his first day out he had niggas still sitting him on a throne like a boss. "Thank you for helping him, baby. You're too much, boy."

He smiled and showed those pretty white teeth. "It's nothing I wouldn't do for you, Bella. Plus, he was a good nigga to my family, so he got it."

I lay back in the tub, letting the hot water sooth my aches and pains away. I was so glad Drew got what he had coming, but I was sad for his daughter who had to be there to witness it. I didn't give a fuck about Asia either. That bitch wanted my life so bad she got it and I knew he was beating the shit out of her too. I couldn't believe he tried to tell me that he was changed and that he wasn't the same person. No less than three minutes later his true form emerged, and he was right back to being who he always been. Now he was nothing and that was fine with me. I wanted to ask Domo what he had for my father, but I knew my place and I didn't want to piss him off by being to nosey. I just let it go.

***

After three weeks we found out all our fucking and hard work had not been in vain. I was pregnant and he was so happy he jumped in the air when the test read positive. I was kind of having mixed emotions because he had to go to an appointment with Diamond today and he wanted me to go with him. I didn't want to, but since I didn't want them alone, I agreed. When we got to the clinic she was smiling until she saw me with him.

"What the fuck is she doing here?"

I snapped my neck.

"Bitch, this my husband. He wanted me here so that's where the fuck I am."

She rolled her eyes and looked at Domo. "You can go back but she needs to stay the fuck where she at."

He got close to her ear, but I could hear what he

was saying. "Bitch, if you ever disrespect my wife again, I will fuck you up and not think twice. She can go wherever the fuck she wants, and I dare you to say something. I wanted ya'll to at least be civil, but you still mad because I wouldn't wife your stank ass so I guess I was wrong."

She sat there like a child. She saw the people looking at her and she decided to get balls. "Well fuck you too then, nigga. I don't need you to wife me; look what you did to her with me. Only a dumb bitch would take a nigga back after getting another bitch pregnant. I see why you could easily step out on this bitch. You can get the fuck out too."

Domo grabbed her around the throat. I was embarrassed by what she said because people were staring and looking at us.

"Who the fuck you talking to? You think I won't snap your fucking neck right here in this waiting room?"

I pulled his arm because she was pregnant, and I didn't want him to get in trouble.

"Sir, you need to leave before I call the police." A nurse spoke up.

He let her go and grabbed my hand and we walked out.

"Fuck that bitch. Let's go see how they coming along with the house." He opened my door and I got in. I knew it was a bad idea to bring me.

When we got to the house it was complete on the outside. They said we had two more weeks to go for it to be complete. We couldn't go in but I loved it already.

"Thank you, baby, for all this. It's beautiful."

"You're beautiful, that's just a house but you're a queen." He lifted my chin and planted a kiss on my lips. He put his hand on my stomach though it was still flat he put his face to it. "I can't wait to see you, whatever you are."

And he kissed it.

"Awwww. Look at you, Daddy."

He laughed me off and we went to the mall and he was already picking up baby stuff, for a boy of course.

"You don't even know what it is yet."

He threw some blue onesies in the cart. "I know it's a boy. Just trust me, woman." He smacked by butt and we kept shopping. He got a phone call and it was pretty heated. Somebody was all type of bitches and hoes.

"Yeah and when he come make sure he wearing a suit because his ass is done." He hung up.

"Who was that?" I asked, getting concerned.

"That hoe, Diamond, playing with her brother life. Said she was sending him to see me."

I shook my head. I know him well and I knew this wouldn't play out in her or his favor.

"Let get this shit and head home. I gotta make some calls."

When I got home, I was sitting there looking at all the shit we just bought. Domo was out back on the phone, so I decided to call my father to see what he was up to.

"Hola, bonita. Que pasa?"

Sometimes he just spoke Spanish and since I spoke it he wanted me to as well. I preferred English. "Hola Papa. What are you up to?"

I could hear a girl's voice in the background. "I have a little company, mi Amor. I will call you a little later." He hung up without even saying bye.

Old perv, I laughed to myself. Domo came in the room and he went to his closet and grabbed something.

"I gotta roll, baby. I'll be back as soon as I can." He kissed me and rolled out.

What the fuck was that about? I asked Satia to make

me one of her infamous paninis. She of course said no problem and I was eating good as shit. I lay on the bed watching TV until I fell asleep. He came in around one a.m. and he went straight to the basement. I didn't know what the hell he was doing so I stayed upstairs in bed. I heard him moving shit around and I could hear the door opening and closing. What the hell was he doing?

The next two weeks were hell. I was sick all the time and I was throwing up so much I started to lose weight. Domo was perfect. He was waiting on me hand and foot and I hadn't even grown a belly yet. I loved that man and I could tell he loved me just as much if not more. He even stopped using that white because he said he needed a clean mind to make sure he was being the best husband and father he could be. I was proud of him for stepping up and making me and our unborn child his priority. I was packing up because we were moving into our new house in Biscayne Bay. It sat right on the water and we had a beautiful view of the bay. I was overexcited. All I ready had to pack was the clothes and shoes because we were keeping this house we would just use it when we came to south beach. I had just finished with the shoes, which was boxes upon boxes. I was worn out. I fell asleep before even having dinner.

Chapter 9

I woke up to a loud crashing sound and I heard yells and I couldn't make out what they were saying. Domo was gone. I saw the bedroom door fly open and guns were pointed in my face.

"Get down! Get the fuck down!"

I climbed out the bed and got on the floor. They handcuffed me and started ransacking the house. I was sitting in the police car watching them take things out the house and bagging it with what looked like evidence bags. They drove me off and I was wondering where the fuck Domo was. I sat in the police station for hours and I didn't want shit but to go home.

"Is this her?" a black guy wearing a shabby suit said, sitting next to me on a bench.

"I'm agent Morrison with the Major Case Squad."

I looked at him, wondering why I should care. "Ok, and that means what to me?"

He laughed and looked at the other cop. "Well, what it means is that your husband Dominic Birkdale, is wanted for the murder of Thomas Sidwell and Antionette Sidwell. Antionette Sidwell was a state witness who we wanted to testify to get an indictment on your husband."

"I never heard of any of these people except my husband who I'm sure didn't kill anyone. Can I have a lawyer please?" He pulled out a picture and I didn't recognize the man, but when he showed me the picture of the dead pregnant woman, I cover my hand with my mouth, and I was mortified. Diamond had a large hole in her head, and she was laid out on the floor. He wouldn't kill her while she was pregnant with his baby, would he?

"Why would you show me that?"

He pushed the pictured back in the folder. "She worked at your husband's strip club and we believe he found out she dropped dime on him and that's why he did it. We don't know why he would kill the brother. We also found out through Ms. Sidwell in her testimony that she was having your husband's child."

That shit stung like a bee. I looked at him and said, "Lawyer."

My father always told me to always ask for a lawyer as soon as they started to talked to you. I was sitting there trying to figure out what the hell just happened. Domo was gone. Did he know they were coming and just left me? I heard him moving shit around. I wondered if he was packing up and leaving. When they gave me my phone call, I called my father. He said he would send a lawyer right away and not to say a word, but I already knew that. A few hours later I was walking out a free woman. I wasn't under arrest they just wanted to see if I knew anything about where Domo was or if he did the shit. I caught a ride home with the lawyer and when I got there it was completely destroyed. They ripped open the couches and broke held the shit in there. There where holes in the walls and even the mattresses where tore the hell up. I didn't have a phone or anything. It looks like they grabbed it with the rest of the shit thinking it was Domo's. I could hear crying and I walked into the kitchen and Satia had her head on the counter.

Mrs. Birkdale, the house is destroyed. Where is Mr. Birkdale?" I shrugged my shoulders and looked around and my once beautiful home. Satia jumped when her phone started ringing. She pulled it out and answered it. She gave me the phone and I looked at the number and it was blocked.

"Hello?" I timidly greeted the caller.

"Baby, are you ok?" I started crying as soon as I hear Domo's voice.

"Oh my God, where are you? How could you just leave me like that?"

"I didn't want to. That was the only way I could protect you. I didn't do that shit, baby. I own my shit, but somebody setting me up baby. I just don't know who. That bitch Diamond went to the police after that shit at the clinic and told them I had drugs in the house and that I was a moving weight. They know who my father is so now I'm on their list of niggas. I knew about that part of it but since I'm not a dumb nigga the house was clean. This morning I was on the way back to the house with some breakfast and I saw them swarm the house, so I just drove by. Now, I hear they want me for killing the bitch and her brother. I swear I didn't do that shit, mamí."

If he would have never fucked that hoe, we wouldn't be in this shit.

"Where are you? You can't just leave me here, Dominic."

"Baby calm down. I will come for you, just go to the new house and I will send for you. I can't tell you where I am right now. Just trust me. There will be something in the kitchen for you when you get there. I love you, baby."

I was in tears; he was gone and he wanted me to just

stay here until when?

"I love you too but —"

He had hung up.

I handed Satia her phone. "You can start coming to the new house starting tomorrow," I said to Satia.

"Ok, Mrs. Birkdale."

"Call me Bella, Satia." I smiled at her, trying not to show how broken I was.

I went upstairs and I looked at all the stuff we just brought for the baby and it was scattered with everything else. I gathered some stuff and just decided to leave everything there. I wasn't in any mood to move shit. I just grabbed some clothes and my toothbrush and left. Satia left before me so I locked up and got in my car and headed to Biscayne. I tried to reason with my emotions because I couldn't understand why he wouldn't tell me where he was. Why couldn't I come today? I got to the house and broke down when I went inside. It was incredible and I didn't have my husband here to see this with me. We had already gotten it furnished and I couldn't be as happy as I wanted to be.

I went to the bedroom and saw that there was a box sitting on the bed that had my name on it. I opened it had a gun, a cell phone, a passport, a credit card and a title to a Lear Jet in my name. What the fuck was all of this? The note said to plug the phone up and wait. I did just that. It never rang, though. I lay in bed the whole day not doing anything but peeing and waiting for Domo to call me. Days passed and I still heard nothing from him. I was in a deep depression and I couldn't shake the shit. My father told me he was okay and that he was sure he would come for me but it was probably too risky with the police looking for him. I wasn't trying to hear that shit though. I wanted my man back and I had no idea how to reach him. He must have dumped his phone because it was going straight to voice-mail. I had no choice but to take care of myself for the sake of the baby.

I had a doctor's appointment today and I wished I wasn't going alone. I cheered up a little when the doctor found the baby's heartbeat. I left the clinic happy knowing all the stress hadn't affected the baby. I was headed to work when I realized I didn't bring the phone with me and I didn't want to miss if Domo called. I sped home to grab my phone. When I got there, I went and checked and I still had nothing. I threw it against the wall and sat on the bed, worn out from driving myself crazy. I picked the phone up and left to go to the spa. I still had to run the business no matter how fucked up I was feeling. When I got there, Lex, my front desk receptionist, told me I had somebody waiting for me in the office. I was hoping it was Domo surprising me. I messed with my hair and got ready to walk in. When I entered, I was disappointed that it wasn't Domo, but Asia.

"What the fuck are you doing here?" I said, about to slap the shit out of her ass for even showing up at my place of business.

"Chill out. I just want to talk to you about something."

Now what the hoe had to talk to me about? "What do you want Asia? I got shit to do," I said, standing instead of sitting just in case I had to rush the bitch.

"I think you owe me a lot due to the fact that it's your fault Jasmine's father is dead," she said, referring to her and Drew's daughter.

"Bitch, bye. If you came here to try to get money your ass is sadly mistaken. Why the fuck would I give you shit but a swift kick to the face for what the fuck you did? Go kill yourself, bitch. Get the fuck out my office."

She sat forward. "Please don't make me call the police and tell them to start looking for Drew. Your father will be right back in jail fucking with me."

This bitch did not just threaten my father. I knew what I had to do. I was no longer going to cry about my problems; I was going to deal with it.

"You know what? You right, Asia. I got something for you. Call me tonight and we can meet up somewhere. I guess I owe Jasmine that much," I said playing the role.

"I knew you would see it my way. Play with me if you want, Bella, and your father and your man gonna be on lockdown."

Now the bitch bringing my nigga into it. She had it coming. I wasn't about to let the bitch hurt my family. I was only doing what my father or Domo would do. I went home and grabbed the gun and checked to see if it was loaded. I waited until about seven to see if she would call. I told my father to come over and he showed up right away.

"Hey, baby girl."

I let him walk pass and I closed the door then locked it. "Papa, Asia came to my spa today and said we needed to pay her to keep quiet about what happened with Drew."

He laughed and shook his head. "When will these bitches ever learn? Don't worry about it, baby girl. I got it handled. She should know better than to fuck with me."

I pulled the gun from behind my back and he looked surprised. "I'm not worried. I told her to meet me tonight and I was going to handle the bitch."

He clapped his hands together like he was honoring me. "My baby doll is growing up. You never let anybody threaten your family. Have you talked to Dominic?"

I shook my head.

"I'm sure he will call soon. I had to send for your mother once[LB50] because I left in hurry trying to get away from the Dominican police. I came here and I got her as soon as things cooled down. She was pissed too, just like you are. Just understand that men who do what we do sometimes do things you may not understand but it's because we love you." I smiled and he laid me on his chest and kissed my forehead.

"Papa, I been meaning to ask. That night when you came home I heard Domo tell you he had said something for you. What was it?"

"I'm back in. All I know is being a dope dealer and that's what I'm going to die doing. He hooking me up for the low until I can run shit again."

"Papa, I don't want you to get locked up."

He grinned at me. "I will be fine, Bonita. Are you ready to do what you said? If you're not I can send somebody to handle it for you."

I put my gun in my purse. "I think I need to handle this bitch myself. We got unfinished business anyway."

He kissed my cheek and left. Asia's greedy ass called me soon after he left. I told her to meet me at the house Drew and I once shared. She told me she was now living there and that would be fine. I thought it would be a vacant, but I guess not. I drove there slightly uneasy because I never killed anybody before. I parked a few blocks away and walked the rest, when I got to the front door, I took a deep breath before ringing the bell.

She answered it with a cigarette in her hand and she blew the smoke in my face.

"Damn, took you long enough."

I looked around for Jasmine and she wasn't around.

"Where's Jasmine?"

She turned around and smacked her teeth. I looked around at my old house of horrors. It was still nice, but it smelled like stale Newport's and weed.

"She at my mother's house, like you give a fuck. Where's the money?"

I had enough of this bitch. I went in my purse and pulled the .22. Out. Her eyes bugged out her face.

"I don't hear your smart as mouth now, Asia. Where all the good shit you was talking at the office, huh?"

She had her hands up. "I didn't mean shit by it. I would have never told the police."

I raised the gun to her head. "Bitch, you fucked me over one to many times. You have the balls to threaten my father and my nigga?"

She was shaking her head no. "Please, Bella..."

I fired one shot and I missed her. I went to fire again and was lifted off the ground and the gun was taken from me. I saw five guys I didn't recognize standing in the living room.

"Oh my God, thank you for saving me. This crazy bitch tried to shoot me!" Asia screamed out.

One of the men walked over to her and kicked her in the face and she fell on the floor. The person who was holding me put me down. It was Lando, Domo's right hand, the one who helped him in the basement with the guy.

"What the hell are y'all doing?" I asked.

"Word got back to Domo about you getting yourself into trouble."

How the fuck could he have known what was happening? I think I was more pissed because he could contact him, but not me. I heard Asia screaming and I turned around to see one of the men between her legs fucking her.

The other guy was sticking his dick into her mouth. She had a pair of vice grips on both of her nipples. After the one guy got off her another one flipped her over and shoved his dick into her ass. I closed my eyes tightly.

"Bella please help me!" she screamed out.

"You might want to leave. Domo want it slow and painful. You got a ride outside to take you to the airport and don't worry about going home; we grabbed what he told us to. I'm gonna drive your car home as soon as we done here."

I walked out the door and saw a limo sitting there. Airport?

"Mrs. Birkdale, you can come with me," the driver said, holding the door open.

I got in and saw the box that had all the stuff Domo left for me. I was so excited he was finally bringing me to be with him, wherever that was. The ride to the airport was haunted by Asia's screams and the images of her being gang raped in my mind. She brought it on herself. You don't fuck with nobody's family. I gave her a chance to walk away in my office. I had to let the shit out of my mind and move on. When I got to the airport, the cell phone finally rung. I answered it so quick I almost dropped it.

"Baby, is this you?" I yelled into the phone.

"How you doing, mamí?"

I missed his voice so much and it sounded so good. "Why the hell haven't you called me? I'm pregnant and you just cut me off."

He ignored the statement. "I just need to you to go to that counter that we went to when we went to Brazil." I looked for the counter and walked up to it. "Hand her your D.L." I did what he told me. She told me to go to Gate Z8.

"I missed you so much. You could have at least

texted me or something. I mean damn," I said, ready to curse him out.

"Babe, I was trying to wait until shit died down, but when I get calls that you're out here trying to assassinate bitches I had to grab you before you did some wild shit. Just go to the gate and when you get there call me to tell me what you think."

He then hung up. I sat at the window because the jet had not pulled in yet. I texted Peaches to tell her I was going away for a while. I turned to look out the window and I was floored. A pink jet with my name going across the side in white large letters. There was a picture of my face at the end of my name. They told me I could board and when I got on there, I almost shed a tear. It was all white and pink. The walls and carpet were white, and the furniture was pink. It was setup just like Domo's and it had a bedroom just like his. I took out the phone and called Domo.

"You are too much!" I screamed in the phone when he answered.

"I take it you love it?" he chuckled into the phone.

"I love it. Thank you so much, baby. You never cease to amaze me." I sat down and put my seat belt on.

"Come to daddy, baby. Enjoy your flight. I love you, Bella," he said in his deep, smooth sexy ass voice.

"I love you too, boo, but where am I flying to?" I asked still not sure where I was going.

"See you when you get here."

Then he hung up. When we got into the air, I was curious as to where we were going. I hit the button for the stewardess.

"Yes, Mrs. Birkdale?"

"Where are we going?" I asked.

"To take you to your husband," was all she said.

Domo must have told them not to say anything. I turned on the TV and it had cable channels. This shit was dope. After we got steady in the air, I went to the fridge and it was packed. I grabbed a yogurt and a hot pocket. I put it in the microwave. After 6 hours I got bored and went into the room and turned the TV on. I watched *Good Times* until I fell asleep. When I woke up, we were still flying. This nigga must be way the fuck out. I went to the closet to get a towel so I could shower. When I opened it, there was a gorgeous line of clothes. I looked at some of the price tags and one of the shirts cost over three grand. He went all out. I opened the drawer on the bottom and it was filled with shoes neatly lined up. I picked out a Puma purple and white sweat suit and the matching pair of Puma tennis shoes. I got in the shower, dressed, and went to the front of the plane and sat in a plush leather seat. I saw ground and I couldn't make out where we were. I started to see the top of buildings, I saw the Eiffel Tower and I started jumping around in my seat. Oh my God! I always wanted to go to Paris. He was here this whole time. When we landed, I was so ready to get off and see Domo. He was full of surprises. When I was getting off the plane, the cell phone Domo gave me rung.

"I'm glad you made it okay," he said in the phone.

"Baby, I can't believe I'm in France."

"Well believe it, girl. Go to the pickup spot."

I looked at the signs and everything was in French. I just walked through until I saw signs in English. I walked toward the arrow that said "transport." I went outside and waited for the next move from him.

"Is there a limo coming, or something?"

"You think I wasn't picking you up myself?"

I turned around and my baby was standing there

looking fine as ever. I jumped into his arms and her swung me around. I kissed him all over his face. He put me down and I punched him in the arm. "Don't ever do that shit to me again." I looked around and was fascinated by my surroundings.

"Let's go, mamí. I got plans for you."

I got into the Orange and Black Charger he had double-parked in front of the airport.

"I missed you so much baby," I said with my hand behind his head.

"I missed you, too, girl. I'm going to show you how much when we get out this car."

I blushed at the thought of us making love. "So what have you been doing?"

I loved how the streets and buildings looked. I saw fresh bread and fruit stands; it was so different from home.

"I started something slight out here. I got in touch with a nigga out here who moving good dope and when I get back home, we going to do business. So, I been making moves and shit." He was never not working I see.

"Well, where are we staying at?"

He smiled at me and drove faster. "Just enjoy the ride baby."

We pulled up in front of a small row house on a tiny street. It didn't look like much from the outside, but the inside was luxury all the way. He couldn't help but be flashy I saw.

"So, what's the plan?" I asked sitting on the chair by the kitchen door.

"I don't really know. I need to find a way to make them charges go away. I know we can't stay here forever, but I don't think we have a choice until I can get something done with this bogus ass shit," he said, pouring a cup of juice handing it to me.

"Did you do it? You can tell me the truth."

He shook his head no. "I didn't kill them, why wouldn't I own it, especially to you? You seen me drop muhfuckas; ain't no need to lie, Bella."

"Ok, then. I guess we need to come up with a plan. Who you think setting you up?" I asked taking a sip of my juice.

"I don't know, but I got people on it."

I let the subject go. "So, what are we going to do first?"

He walked up to me and kissed me. "First you can go upstairs and get naked so I can wear that pussy out and then we can talk about later."

I jumped up, went upstairs, and got naked like he asked. I looked around the bedroom and it looked old fashioned but chic. I waited for him to come up and when he finally did he was carrying a tray. He sat it down and it had chocolate and strawberries on it.

"Lay down." I did as I was told and laid across the bed. He stuck his hand in the chocolate and rubbed it across my pussy lips. He ran his tongue along it, and I shivered at his touch.

"I missed this pretty pussy, baby," he said, parting my pussy lips with his tongue and pushed it inside of me.

"I missed you too, daddy," I said, holding on to his head. He picked up a strawberry, dipped it in chocolate, and circled my pussy hole with it. Then he pushed it inside me and leaving some out so he could bite it and pushed it in and out of me. He took it out and ate it.

"I can eat this pussy all day girl." He was licking the chocolate out of me and I was ready to cum, but he stopped.

"Stop playing, boy."

He started licking again and wiggled his tongue on my clit and I came super hard, curling my toes and trying not to burst open. I wanted to try to top him, so I sat up and pulled his pants down, I rubbed chocolate on his balls and licked them clean. I took his dick in both my hands and I twirled it and sucked the tip. I went down as far as possible and he pushed it hard and made me gag.

"Open that throat for me, baby."

I opened my throat until I got as much of his dick in my mouth as I could. I had tears coming down because I was gagging so much. His dick was too big to deep throat.

"Stand up and grab your ankles. Don't move, Bella."

He walked away and came back with a scarf and a belt. He wrapped the belt around my ankles and hands, looped it, and tightened it. Domo gripped my hips and pushed into my waiting pussy. I was dripping wet and needed this dick. The position hurt, but it was a good pain. He was wearing my ass out and my legs had buckled and he stood me back up.

"Don't move unless I tell you to."

We stayed in that position until my calves were burning. He finally released me and he put me on top and I rode him until we both came.

"Now take me to explore Paris," I said, getting up with baby deer legs.

I was wobbling and I shook my legs until they came back.

"Yeah, I see this daddy dick got your ass weak at the knees," he laughed, standing up and pushing me into the bathroom.

"One more round and we can go."

I smiled and we got into the shower and he hit it out

the park again. It felt good to have my man back.

We saw some sights and went jewelry shopping. Dom said he wanted to refresh my ring. The people were okay but some were just rude as shit. I couldn't help but snap on some people who bumped me while walking down the street. They don't even say "excuse me." I wished he had chosen the Islands; I could use some drinks and a relaxing beach. I sat on the balcony and watched the small cars and people walk the streets and I smiled. This nigga was international as shit; I was impressed he was so well traveled. He always had to find a way to do business though; there was nothing wrong with an ambitious nigga and that he was.

"I need you to pick out a dress because we're going to a party tonight for my new hook up's daughter."

I didn't feel like going anywhere. "Do I have to? I can sit here and watch French *Family Guy*," I laughed, watching the channel and not understanding shit they were saying. I was reading the captions.

"No, let's get you something. You can wear that new necklace I got you."

I gave in and we went to a boutique and picked out a purple tight-fitting ball gown. I didn't really like the cut of it. People walking by the boutique window were staring so I must have looked good. I was glad my glad my stomach wasn't out already big, I didn't want to look like a pregnant dolphin. I picked up some diamond encrusted heels and a matching clutch. All of the shit came up to twelve grand and Domo swiped his card like it was nothing. We went home and ate fish and potatoes. It wasn't my first choice, but the food selection was a little different here. I made a mental note to ask him to swing by Burger King on the way to wherever we were going. We got into our car and we drove off. I notice as we hit turn after turn the houses seemed to get a little bigger. We landed in front of a lovely mansion that looked more like an older castle. When we walked in it was more people speaking English than French. Domo introduced me to a few people and the birthday girl walked up to us.

"Bonjour, Dominic," she said, gliding up and putting her hand out for him to kiss. She didn't even acknowledge I was there until Domo said something.

"This is my wife, Bella."

She smiled and turned back to him. "I have some things to discuss with you, in private." She cut her eyes at me.

"Anything you can say to me you can say in front of my wife Celia." She looked crushed. Something wasn't right. I bent over in his ear.

"You fucked this bitch?" he kept his eyes ahead.

"We will talk about it later," he said through gritted teeth.

"No, were talking about the shit now," I said, talking louder. He pulled me by the arm into another room.

"It was business, baby. She the plug now and her father wants me to deal with her."

I looked as if he insulted my intelligence. "You see how she just disrespected me? That's because you did it when you fucked her and now, she thinks it's ok. What part of the business is that? You left me so you could come fuck some stuck-up ass French bitch, for what?"

He yoked me by the arm and got close to my ear. "Do you want me to kill her baby?" he asked looking at me seriously.

"Why would you do that? She ain't the one who's married."

"Because I don't want any bitch or nigga to disrespecting my wife. You said you felt disrespected, right? He pulled the gun out the back of his pants."

He was fucking crazy. He's the one that fucked her and was wrong.

"I want you to stop disrespecting me. Are you going to kill yourself?"

He gave me a stare that told me to shut my mouth now. "I fucked her so I could make her happy and get this shit on lock. If I had the daughter of the biggest drug dealer in France in my pocket, then I could start my international shit. I'm sorry, baby, but in this shit you gotta make sacrifices."

I tried to fight back the tears. I remembered what my mother told me. I thought about everything he gave me and knew I couldn't get this with any normal ass nigga. I still couldn't just let him fuck who he pleased. "Well maybe I should go get myself a nigga to fuck while you busy giving my dick to every bitch who can take it."

That wasn't a smart thing to say. He grabbed the back of my neck but not tightly. He pulled me to him and started to rock like we were dancing.

"Don't make me fuck you up for talking stupid, Bella. I don't ever want to hit you, but if I ever found out anybody touched my wife, I don't know what I would do."

I can't believe him; he can just fuck whoever and I'm supposed to just wait around to be an idiot? "Kill her. If you don't, I will," I said, walking away from him and going back into the party.

I saw him go talk to her and she looked around until she found me and gave me a smirk like she had won. I didn't want him to touch anybody but me. I didn't want to sacrifice our intimacy so he could be an international connect. I was going to make some things clear. I wondered what was taking him so long. I walked to the back where I see them go and I check a few bedrooms. I didn't see them. The final one I went to; I knew I had the right one. I couldn't believe he was fucking this bitch while I sat out here waiting for him to kill her ass. I burst in the room, and he had his hands around her throat. I came in and closed the door.

"What the hell is taking so long? I thought you were fucking her again."

She reached her hand out to me and you could see the veins ruptured in her eyeballs. I didn't feel anything but anger. I knew he didn't take me serious enough. I didn't have time for anymore bullshit or I was going to go fucking crazy.

"This is all your fault. Keep your fucking dick in your pants, Domo." I said, after he dropped her body.

"I got you, baby. I'm trying to make us King and Queen of this shit." He came kissing my neck.

"I don't want you to fuck other girls. It hurts me and I don't want to feel like a fool again."

"I'm not trying to do that, baby." He rubbed his hand over my belly as she lay dead on the floor.

"Let's get the fuck out of here before somebody see us," I said, opening the door and checking the hallway. We walked down the hallway and when I heard somebody coming, I quickly grabbed him, and we kissed like we were just drunk lovers. We weren't paid any attention. We said bye quickly, went to the valet and waited for our car. I heard a scream and our car pulled up just in time. They must have found the bitch. Who the fuck was I know? Murder was normal, my nigga cheated, and I wasn't as hurt as I should be. I was becoming somebody else.

I was becoming numb to everything and I felt myself turning into my mother.

Chapter 9

After two months of hiding in Paris, I was homesick and wanted to go back to Miami. My stomach had grown and I had a small baby bump now. I enjoyed the time we had here, but I wanted to at least go back for a visit. Domo had been talking to a lawyer who told him he thinks there was no warrant when they entered my home and he also said they didn't have a solid case for the murders. He said it would be best if he turned himself in and let them try the case. I didn't want him to be locked up. I mean what if he didn't win? We discussed it and decided that it was a chance we had to take to get back home. He was being stubborn about it until he got a call from his aunt called and said his mother had come to get his sister. He was infuriated. I didn't blame him seeing the condition she was in when I first met her. He called his lawyer to see if he turned himself in could he get a bond. The lawyer said it was possible because his record was clean. Domo must have been very smart not to ever have gotten caught doing anything illegal. He made a decision to try and clear himself and we were set to go home. Domo wanted to take his jet and leave mines in a hangar. He said he could have it flown in if I wanted, but it wasn't like I would be flying often so I told him he could leave it. The day we flew back was so miserable because I knew he would be leaving me again once he turned himself in. I was so scared because if he didn't win his case then what. Once we landed he called the lawyer and told him he would meet him at the police headquarters.

"Listen, babe, do you remember where I took you to get my sister?" I nodded my head yes. "I need you to go get her and take her home with you. Don't worry about me, ok? I'm asking you to do it because I don't want her to see me going into a police station to get locked up, plus I trust you and I know you will be good to her."

I put my head down and felt a tear slide down my cheeks. He took his thumb and wiped it away.

"You coming back, right?" I asked, just looking for a glimmer of hope.

"You know I am, Bella. Love you boo." He kissed me and got out the car.

"I love you too, baby." I watched him walk inside the building and I took a deep breath to be strong. I chose this nigga so I gotta deal with this like a boss nigga's wife. I drove to his mother's house and she was sitting outside talking to another woman who looked like she was on that shit. They were laughing and cackling on the porch smoking cigarettes. I walked straight up to her.

"Domo sent me. I came to get Marion."

She looked at me with glassy red eyes. "You must be his flavor of the month. He like y'all uppity bitches, don't he?" She smacked hands with the other crack head.

"I ain't no flavor of the month; I'm his wife. Now take your raggedy crackhead ass in there and get Marion before I get rude."

She got up and took her shoes off and came over and

threw a punch and fell on the ground. While I was laughing, her friend got up and caught me in the face. I pulled my mace and maced her filthy ass. I ain't have time to beat these fiends. I needed to do what Domo asked and get his little sister. When I went in there was no trace of her. I went into the back and I could hear her crying. When I opened the door to the room she had duct tape over her mouth and she was tied up in the corner. I ran over to her and started to untie her. I was knocked against the head with something heavy. I was dazed for a minute and I saw Domo's mother standing there with an end table leg.

"Yeah, I told you I had something for you, bitch," she said, laughing like this shit was over.

I reached into my purse and pulled out the .22 and pointed it at her. "And I got something for you, too."

Her eyes grew wide and I popped her in the shoulder and she fell down screaming. I finished untying Marion and I got her the hell out of there. I put her in the back and I got in the front.

"Put your seat belt on, sweetie." I said, nervous because I just shot somebody. I hoped she wouldn't have called the police and I hoped she was scared of Domo enough not to do it. She didn't know he was locked up and I didn't want her to know out of fear she would retaliate. I drove to the Kmart and I picked up clothes that looked like her size. I got her some little girl cartoon body wash she asked for and I also got some hair lotion and berates for her hair. When I got to the house, I washed her up, shampooed her hair, and dressed her.

"Where's my big brother, Bella?" she asked, eating her chicken nuggets.

"He had something to do? He will be home, ok?"

She nodded her head up and down. "Ok. Can we eat

ice cream now?"

I smiled and made her a bowl of chocolate ice cream with fudge. The doorbell rung and I wondered who the hell that could be. When I went to answer it I saw Peaches outside with the kids. I swung the door open.

"Hey, boo!" I said kissing her on the cheek.

"Wassup, bitch. I was in the area and decided to slide by. I drove by to see if you had come home yet. I forgot what time you said you was landing." She looked a little out of it.

"Oh, well yeah I'm home. You good?"

She smiled and I saw the tears building in her eyes. "No, Bizzy is getting worse. He started drinking a lot and doing more blow since Drew died. I can't even fight him back anymore sis."

I came over and hugged her. "Why don't you just leave? You helped me. Take your own advice, Peaches."

She wiped her eyes. "I am. I got me and the kids an apartment and I'm moving Saturday when he out of town at his mother's house. I gotta go."

I gave her kids some ice cream and we sat in the living room.

"You know Domo turned himself in today."

She shook her head. "Damn, I know that shit gotta be tough. Have you heard from him yet?"

"No, not since I dropped him off. I'm going to call and see what they tell me." She gave me the number; she knew it by heart because of all the times Bizzy got locked up. I called and was on hold forever. A woman finally answered rudely and I asked about Domo. She said he was still being processed. Damn, I wish I had that lawyer's number to see what the fuck was going on. I chilled with Peaches a little longer and she told me she needed to head home.

"Be safe, girl." She gave me a hug.

"I will."

She rounded up her kids and left. I'll be glad when I know she safe and away from that nigga. I put Marion to bed in the guest room and I went to my room and waited to hear something. I started dosing off and then I jumped back up so I wouldn't miss him if he called. I waited as long as I could until I fell asleep. I don't know long I was out before my phone was ringing. I answered the phone.

"Hello."

"Hey, baby. They said they can't get me in front of a judge until tomorrow."

I sighed. I didn't want to spend a night without him. "What time does court start tomorrow?"

"I don't want you in no courtroom baby, not with my little sister at that."

I exhaled heavily. "This is bullshit. Why the fuck can't I come?"

"Who are you talking to Bella? You need to remember who you are talking to. You heard what the fuck I said. Don't bring my sister into no damn courthouse. Now get some sleep for the baby. I will get my lawyer to call you tomorrow after court. Love you."

He hung up and I laid down. I didn't get much sleep. I tossed and turned until I passed out. I felt myself rocking back and forth and I opened my eyes to see Marion jumping on my bed.

"I want some cereal!" she screamed.

I went downstairs and went into the cabinet to get some fruit loops for her.

Satia cleaned the fridge and brought some groceries in for me yesterday thank God. I poured her bowl and I waited patiently to hear from Domo's lawyer. Once one o'clock rolled around, I was tired of watching my phone. My phone rung and I answered it on the first ring.

"Mrs. Birkdale, I was calling to let you know Dominic has been granted bail. If you want to come posts its two hundred thousand.

"Ok, I'm going to a bondsman right now."

I handled my hygiene and put on a pair of maternity jeans and a t-shirt. I got Marion cleaned up and dressed and I went to post his bond. I went home because I knew Domo was serious about me staying away from the court and the jail. I was cooking dinner and couldn't help but wonder what was taking him so long. I had just put Marion's plate down when I heard the alarm chime telling me somebody entered the front door. I ran out to the foyer and he was standing there smiling with his arms open.

"I was waiting baby. What took so long?"

He bear hugged me kissing me and putting me down. "They took forever letting me go. I have to go back next month." I wouldn't worry about next month. I was happy to have him here right now.

"I made some spaghetti. You hungry?"

He smacked his teeth "You know I'm hungry."

We sat down and ate. We didn't even have sex that night; he just held me and rubbed my belly. I heard his phone go off and he picked it up and answered it.

"Yeah." He was listening to what the other person said. "I can come through tomorrow but I'm in for the night, bruh. I just got home and y'all niggas wanna fuck up now?" He hung up and put his arm back around me.

"You good, baby?" I asked looking at the TV.

"Yeah, them niggas fucked up the count now they saying some of our clients gonna be short. They better re-count before some fingers come up missing." He wasn't joking either.

"Baby something happened when I went to Get Marion."

He continued to rub my stomach. "What?" he asked, kissing the back of my neck.

"Your mother had Marion tied up and she hit me with a stick so I shot her."

"Is she dead?" he asked very cool and calm.

"No, I just took Marion and left."

He scrunched his face up. "She had her fucking tied up? You should have killed her ass. You better hope she don't press charges. I would hate to have to kill my own mother."

I didn't want to believe he would kill his own mother. I figured he was just blowing off steam.

Domo didn't go back to run the strip club. Instead, he was starting back at the construction company. I went there one day to see what the assistant looked like. She was an older lady so I felt better about it. I didn't think he was cheating again but I never knew. I jumped right back into work at the spa. We tried not to think about the case and we just enjoyed each other like it was the last time we would see each other. I was heading in the house from picking Marion up from school when my phone started ringing. It was a random number.

"Hello?"

The person hung up. My phone vibrated and a picture came through of me at that moment walking in the house. I looked around but I didn't see anything or anybody looking at me. I hurried Marion inside, and I closed and locked the door. I called out for Domo and he came running down the steps.

"Are you ok, baby?"

My heart was racing. "Somebody called me and then sent me a picture of me."

I showed him the text. He went outside looking around. I guess he didn't see anybody either.

"It's ok, Bella, somebody just playing games. You know I got you. It's cameras all in and out the house. We gonna know if somebody anywhere near us. Fuck 'em. My father wants to meet you. He says he's gonna be in town next week."

That was cool, I guess. He never really talked about him, so I just assumed they never really spoke. I went upstairs and laid down. I had a bad feeling about something, but I didn't know what it was. I was soon to find out.

Domo's court case was a few days away and I was shitting bricks. The lawyer was going to present a case for them to drop the drug charges because their witness was dead, and they found no evidence. He would argue the murder case was bogus and they had no solid proof he was involved. Just the word of some mysterious witness they can't seem to produce to testify. I think he had a good chance of the case being thrown out. I was sitting in the Chic-fil-a eating a spicy chicken sandwich when my phone rung. I saw it was another unknown number, so I hit the end button. I didn't know who the fuck this was playing on my phone, but I was getting tired as shit of it. I went home and waited for Marion to get out of school. I heard a knock on my front door and when opened it nobody was there. I turned to closed the door when was bum rushed.

"I told you I would come back strong, bitch."

I couldn't believe this bitch. "Ja'Tori, have you lost your fucking mind?" I said moving across the floor away from her. I was going into my back pocket for my phone and she kicked my hand.

"Why couldn't you just leave my man alone?" She came down and slapped me across the face. "I had to get rid of that bitch, Diamond. She thought she was having a baby by man. She was sadly mistaken. I had to get rid of the brother because he walked in. Wrong place and time, huh? Dominic didn't know what a good thing he had. Instead he chose a weak little bitch like you? Really?" She kicked my legs.

"You're one sick ass bitch."

She tried to kick me in the stomach, and I blocked her. I clipped her legs from under her and she fell but jumped back up before I could have a chance to get on my feet. She pushed me into the wall, and I hit my head and fell. She was pulling me by my hair, and she tied me up to the step bannister and turned the lights off; I sat on the step wishing Domo would come save me. I knew this simple-minded bitch was going to kill me. If I didn't pick Marion up the school would call Domo and he would come home.

"What is it about you, huh? Your pussy must be made of gold or something." She sat next to me rubbing the gun over my titties. Stopping to rub my nipples. This bitch was insane. "I need to see for myself. I saw your body that day in the room and I saw why he was so attracted to you. I was too jealous to admit it."

She went under my skirt and moved my underwear to the side and started playing with my pussy. She was pushing her fingers in and out of me.

"Is that it? You wanna taste mamas pussy, huh?" I said, playing along and opening my legs.

I was trying to think of a plan. I closed my legs back and she got on the bottom step, sliding my underwear down. She pried my legs open and she went to my pussy.

After taking a long whiff, she dipped her tongue in and out of me. I couldn't help but be sexually excited. I mean somebody was licking my twat and doing a good job at it. I opened my legs wider as she licked and sucked on my clit until I came on her face. She was still digging her tongue in and out my soaked pussy hole. I bounced on her tongue and she was holding my thighs and licking up all my juices. She was sticking her fingers in and out of me. She even ripped the top strap to my dress and started sucking my nipples. I took advantage of the position between my legs and I kneed her in the face and she fell back. I tugged at the ropes around my hands, but they wouldn't come loose. She got up and punched me in the eye.

"You have some good tasting pussy, Bella. I see why he loves to fuck you. Try that shit again, bitch, and I'm going to shoot that little bastard in your stomach first," she said, wiping her face.

She walked off and I could hear water running from the bathroom. I wished I could get to that fucking gun in my purse. I heard a car pull up and she put the gag over my mouth so I wouldn't warn Domo when he came in. When he opened the door he hit the lights he saw me tied up and ran up to me. I saw Marion coming in behind him. I diverted my eyes to Ja'Tori, who was right behind him. It was too late; she hit him over the head with the gun. He was out cold. She went a got a cup of water and threw it on him. Marion was crying in the corner.

"What the fuck are you doing, Ja'Tori?" He shook his head, trying to get himself back together.

"You think you can just dump me, nigga? You got me fucked up and both y'all motherfuckas won't had shit but dirt over your face," she said with tears coming out of her eyes.

"She killed Diamond and her brother, Domo."

He scrunched his eyebrows and looked at her for confirmation.

"Yeah, and that bitch was standing in our way just like this bitch. I don't know, though. I like her Domo," she said, raising the gun to me.

"Stop. Look, baby, forget her. It can be me and you from now on," he said, standing up walking toward her.

She let off a shot and he backed away. "You're lying. You just don't want me to kill this bitch. Kiss me so I can know you mean it."

This bitch was dizzy. He walked over and kissed her on the mouth and she slowly put the gun down, he quickly punched her in the stomach and snatched the gun from her He kept it on her as he untied me. She looked up at him helping me up and showing me love and it infuriated her further. She got up and ran toward us and Domo raised the gun and shot her in the head. Marion started screaming. He untied my arms and held me.

"I have to call the police, baby."

He pulled out his phone and called them. It was self-defense and with the cameras in the house we could also prove she killed Diamond and her brother. I ran over to Marion and I took her into the kitchen. The police came and Domo gave them a copy of the cameras. They said they needed a statement and told us they would get back to us.

"You good, Bella?" Domo asked after everything settled down and the police got the body and collected all their evidence.

"Yeah, I think you need to talk to Marion, though. She is pretty shaken up. He shook his head and walked into her room. I went to ours and sat there thinking of how close I was to being killed. That bitch was crazy as shit and I guess I underestimated her. Domo joined me and he wasn't the least bit rattled about what happened. All he could talk about was that they would have to clear him now. I was happy about that too, but I was still wondering what the fuck could happen next.

***

Shit got pretty normal after that shit with Diamond. It had been over four months later. They dismissed the murder case against Domo but his lawyer said he thinks they are going to be watching him closely because of the suggestion that he was a drug trafficker. Domo still wouldn't fall back. He was still moving good weight and not giving a fuck about the police. He took a trip to Columbia to meet with his plug and he took me with him. I learned all about how his drug empire came to be after it was passed on from his father. I knew his moves; he wanted me to be a queen to his empire, so he was trying to teach me everything he knew. He would let me pick up and choose what punishments he would give to the niggas that were shorting him. I was changing. I don't know if it was good or bad, but I wasn't who I used to be.

Chapter 10

I started noticing Peaches didn't answer the phone like she used to. I couldn't help but feel like I did something wrong to her and I just couldn't figure out what it was. I went to her new place and she answered the door but told me she was busy and closed it. She had something going on and I wished she would tell me what was wrong. I waddled back to the car and I could see her looking out the window. I got in the car and sat for a minute to see what was going on. I didn't have time for this shit. I was seven months pregnant and I needed to get back into the air conditioner. I drove home and called Domo to tell him my appointment was in half an hour. We were getting another sonogram to see what we were having because they couldn't see the baby the first two times. He didn't answer. Instead, he texted me back and said he was in a meeting. Things were going well for us, but I couldn't help but think he was hiding something from me again. I could just feel it.

I went straight to the doctor's office and waited for Domo to come. He still wasn't there when they called me back. I was lying on the bed pissed off that Domo wasn't there. They did the sonogram and I found out we were having a boy. They printed my pictures and I left the office hurt that he missed it. When I got into my car, I saw him pull up. He must have seen me because he parked next to me.

"I'm sorry baby. I got caught up. Did you already get seen?"

I threw the picture into his window. "It's a boy if you give a shit," I said, starting my car.

"Where are you going?"

I looked ahead and drove off. He called my phone and I answered with and attitude. "What?" I said into the phone.

"Pull over right now."

I looked in my rearview mirror and he was behind me. I pulled to the side and he pulled up right behind me. He got out and pulled the handle of my door. I unlocked it and he opened the door and gently helped me out.

"I told you I don't play games, Bella. Who the fuck you think you speeding off on?"

I looked to the ground and he lifted my chin up and made me look at him. "I was mad you missed it," I said biting my bottom lip.

"I wanted to be there, babe. I came as soon as I could get out of the meeting. You know I have a big contract I'm trying to get and that was the money man. I won't miss another one, ok?"   I nodded.

"Ok, I gotta head back to work. I want you to go home and get some rest. I'll home in a few, aight?"

He kissed me and opened my car door. I watched him get into his car and speed off. I went home and asked Satia to make Domo's favorite dish tonight. I knew he was under pressure and I didn't want him to get over worked. I had my lavender massage oil ready to I could oil him down. I lit candles everywhere and I placed rose petals from the door to the kitchen. The house looked sexy. Marion as back in Georgia with their aunt. Domo told her to make sure no matter what his mom said not to let her take Marion. His mother must have feared him or me because she never sent the police. I guess she had gotten the point and decided to leave the shit lone. I sat at the table looking at the time until I saw it was now nine o'clock. I called him and his phone went to voicemail.

"I don't know where you are, but please call me back."

I hung up and sat at the table until eleven rolled around and he still wasn't answering. I let the candles burn out and I smashed the plates on the ground. I went upstairs to the room and as I took of the lingerie my phone lit up.

Hubby: Hey, mamí, I had to make some runs. I will be home as soon as possible.

Fuck that. If he could call he could text.

I called him and he answered right away. "You told me you would be home in a few earlier today. I set up a nice evening for us and I'm sitting here alone looking like a dumbass."

"I didn't know. I had some shit to do. You know how it is baby."

I rolled my eyes because I smelled a rat. "You better not be with no bitch, Domo. I swear I will leave your ass the hell alone."

"Stop talking that crazy shit. I'm on the way home now." He hung up and I waited in bed for him.

He came in and he sat on the bed and I looked straight ahead and the TV. "Don't act like you don't see me here," he said, pushing my leg.

"Leave me alone. You disappointed me all day."

He smacked his teeth and gave me a kiss. I saw he

had glitter on his face. "Why you ain't tell me you went to the strip club, nigga?" He looked confused trying to figure out how I knew he went.

"Well, I own the shit. I can't go there to see what the hell is going on?" I balled my face up and folded my arms.

"Yeah, whatever. You must really think I'm a fool, huh?" I turned over and closed my eyes like I was going to sleep.

"I love you, Bella."

"I love you, too," I said, still facing the wall.

He went and got in the shower then laid down. He was doing something and it hurt me to even think that shit especially since he told me he wasn't going to hurt me again. I was gonna catch his ass and this time I was going to teach him a lesson and really leave for a while. I rubbed my stomach as the baby kicked and hoped to God I was wrong.

I was in my office a week after that suspicious shit with Domo went down when I got a weird call from Bizzy. I don't even know how he got my number, but I recognized his.

"Hey, Bizzy."

He was cursing in the phone and I could barely make out what he was saying. "Tell that nigga he need to watch his back. I don't give a fuck who he is. And tell that bitch, Peaches, she getting fucked up too."

I looked at the phone like it was a snake. "What the fuck are you talking about, Bizzy? You know you don't threaten Domo because you know what he would do," I said reminding him of who my nigga was.

"Oh, I see you still stupid standing by your man, huh?"

I was confused. "I gotta go. You need to stop snorting that shit."

I hung up and I tried to get back to work. It was eating at me, so I called Peaches phone and she didn't answer. I thought should tell Domo what Bizzy had said so I called him too. He answered but he was out of breath.

"Hey, why are you so out of breath?"

He was trying to catch his breath from what I could hear. "I had to run to get my phone. Wassup, baby?"

I heard a woman's voice and the phone hung up. My heart stared beating so fast. I called back more than once, and he didn't answer. I got up and got in my car about to head to his office. I called first and his assistant said he was there. For some reason I decided to go to Peaches house. I was red when I saw Domo's car sitting out front. I walked to the door and I couldn't hear anything inside. I looked through the window and nobody was there. I went around back, and the door was cracked so I walked in and looked around. I could hear the bed squeaking and when I went to the bedroom door I could hear moaning and grunting. I pulled out my gun because if Domo was in their fucking Peaches I was going to kill them both. I kicked the door open and I dropped my mouth when I saw Peaches riding my father.

"What the fuck are you doing?"

They both jumped and got under the covers. I was disgusted at this bitch. That must have been why she was acting so stupid toward me.

"What are you doing in my house, Bella?"

I looked at my father and he looked like a kid with his hand stuck in the candy jar. That must be why Bizzy thought he Domo was in here: because of the car.

"Why do you have Domo's car?" I asked my father.

"He let me use it after I told him I was getting mines customized. I dropped him off at that old house of y'alls so he could get one of his other ones."

I felt so relieved. I was ready to accuse my man of cheating on me. I wondered if he was still there. I left after looking at my father and Peaches in disgust. I drove to South Beach happy I didn't find out the worst about my baby. When I pulled up I saw his car was still there. When I opened the door for some reason the alarm didn't go off and that alarmed me. I heard a bump up stairs and I went into my purse and grabbed my gun again. I couldn't really hear anything until I heard a noise like somebody got smacked. I cracked open the door and my knees got weak; Lex, the front desk receptionist, was riding my husband and he seemed to be in heaven. I let one tear escape my face and I kicked the door open and let the gun give them a round of applause as it clapped and clapped and clapped at their performance.

"No nigga or bitch gonna disrespect your wife. Right, baby?"

───────

To be continued....

Made in the USA
Middletown, DE
29 March 2024

52292798R10085